I0890130

JANE'S ADDICTION: in the Studio

By Jake Brown

'Jane's Addiction: in the Studio'
by Jake Brown

Published by:
Rock 'N' Roll Books,
Nashville, TN
Rocknrollbooks@yahoo.com
www.rocknrollbooks.com
Distributed by: SCB Distributors
www.scbdistributors.com

Associate Publisher: Samuel Sacco
Cover Concept by Jake Brown and Katherine Sandalls
Cover Design by Katherine Sandalls
Book Layout/Design by Byju M. Devan

Library of Congress Cataloging in Publication Date Available
ISBN: 0-9726142-7-6

First Printing, November, 2010

This book is dedicated to... Alex Schuchard for discovering Jane's Addiction with me in the record bins of Vintage Vinyl in 1987. We really did grow into ourselves as musicians via this band throughout junior high from *XXX Live, Nothing's Shocking and Ritual*; and to my dear and longtime friends Chris 'See' Ellauri (www.blessitup.com), Andrew McDermott and Reed Gibbons for our 10th grade year, which was defined musically by *Ritual* in so many magical times that got me through moving in the midst of high school, I'm as grateful to you all as I am the band for giving us the proverbial 'soundtrack of our lives.'

Project Thank You(s): I would first and foremost like to thank Aaron, Gabriel and everyone working at SCB Distributors for doing such an AMAZINGLY-professional job working this title to retail, and publisher Rock 'N' Roll Books for giving this book a home in the first place! FIRST AND FOREMOST, engineer Ronnie S. Champagne for your tireless hours of interviewing for this project, your commitment to the telling of the making of these amazing albums, and your role in helping to change rock history I hope has been duly noted in the course of this narrative; producers Dave Jerden and Bob Ezrin for your participation in the 'Behind the Boards' Rock Producers' anthology and this book by extension; Kelly Wheeler for your interview re the PSI COM days; special thanks to Matthew Ellard for the last minute Deconstruction interview; to Katherine Sandalls for designing the cover; to Byju M. Devan for designing the new layout; Tim Leonhard and Bookmasters for your 100% professional management of pressing duties; auction winner Samuel Sacco; to Sean Peace and David Prohaska at Songvest.com for your help in getting this book to retail!

Personal Thank You(s): My parents, James and Christina Brown, my brother Joshua T. Brown, the extended Brown and Thieme families, Alex and Jackson Schuchard; Andrew and Sarah McDermott; Chris Ellauri (Blessitup.com); Sean and Amy Fillinich; Richard, Lisa and Regan Kendrick; Paul and Helen WATTS; Adam 'The Skipper' Perri; Matt and Eileen Pietz, congrats on the little one; Tim Woolsey; Reed Gibbons; Alexandra 'The

Clown' Federov; Rose Reiter; Aaron 'Whippit' Harmon; Ed Seamen, Rachel, Dave, Larry, Burt Goldstein and everyone else at MVD/Big Daddy Music Distribution who keep Versailles Records' product out there in stores; John Lavallo at Take-Out Marketing; Tony & Yvonne Rose at Amber Books (congrats on beating the big C); Jack David, David, Crissy, Simon, and everyone at ECW Press; Larry, James, Joel and everyone at Arbor Books; Karen Peralta at Rainbow Writing; Lucian Randall et all at John Blake Publishing CO; Richard Anderson et all at Cherry Red Books; Ben Ohmart at BearManor Media; Albert Longden; Lemmy Kilmister, Jasmin St. Claire, Curt and Cris Kirkwood, the Shakur estate, and Tracii Guns for the opportunities to collaborate with you on the study of your creative process or the fuller telling of your amazing life stories; and anyone and everyone else who I have the fortune of being in business with...

TABLE OF CONTENTS

Introduction: Jane's Addiction in the Studio

Part Two: The Birth of Jane's Addiction

Part Three: *Nothing's Shocking*

Part Four: *Ritual De La Habitual*

Part Five: Parting Ways & the birth of Lollapalooza

Part Six: *Deconstruction*

Part Seven: *Porno for Pyros*

Part Eight: *Strays*

Part Nine: Perry Farrell Goes Solo and holds a *Satellite Party*

Conclusion: The Next Generation of Jane's Addiction

"Perry Farrell's role in the alternative rock history book is secure." - Los Angeles Times, 2010

Introduction: Jane's Addiction in the Studio

Jane's Addiction has always centered around the prophetic musical mind of front man Perry Farrell, who the Los Angeles Times has historically hailed as "the consummate master of ceremonies, the ringleader for the circus of the eclectic. His band, Jane's Addiction, embraced Led Zeppelin and X, folk art and tribal culture and made it appeal to football captains and art-house denizens alike. And Farrell gave indie and alternative groups a stadium stage with his brainchild, the concert/happening Lollapalooza," of which Mix Magazine added "at the time...seemed far-fetched, but...actually generated mainstream popularity (for Alternative Rock)...and paved the way for countless other traveling fests." Years before Lollapalooza, when Jane's Addiction's sound was first mesmerizing fans and critics alike, the New York Times excitedly commented of the band's new sub-genre of rock that no one could quite categorize, "it became clear that 'metal' was an inadequate tag for Jane's Addiction's exhilarating fusion of heavy rock, funk, reggae, ethnic influences, tribal rhythms and art rock," while in the same time paying them the traditional respect with their added note that "for all its art-rock complexity, the band seldom sacrifices the raw attack of pure rock-and-roll."

Indeed, Jane's Addiction threw the concept of broadening horizons right out the window, instead creating their own land/soundscape to look out upon, waking up America's youth to the dawn of a new time in music and culture, where the two were intermingled like ecstasy and epic sex, in that mental G-spot where it felt unquestionably good to be bad. Where the confusion of teenage angst for the first time made sense because kids knew how to look at it- Perry Farrell's lyrics gave them a roadmap to not only understand the maze, but also to escape it. A majority questioning is a rebellion answered.

Jane's Addiction wrote a bible for a church of worshipers whose house of God was built on doubt, their sound was the perfect hymn to sooth and heal the wounds of small-minded convention. Jane's sound was an aural acid trip, expanding the boundaries of contrived rectitude until they were stretched too thin to care any more, and finally snapped. The rush of freedom that ensued was as potent as Perry Farrell's heroine, but equally as concise in its point of release, in fact sobering. Jane's Addiction knew just where to prick the needle, just how large a dose was needed to inject into an overly-cautious conscious, desperate to be drugged out of society's brainwash of rules and tools used to manipulate the youth away from their true calling as kids... to be just that, kids. To do wrong because it felt right. The band's music was the morality for that specific society, the sensibility for its doubters, the justification that made it cool to be bad, socially acceptable to be an outcast, because both the bands and their fans were running from the same jailers. And their disciples didn't just come to mass, they came in masses, first to theatres, then auditoriums, and finally to a festival- Lollapalooza. That was the climax of the long, amazing fuck that Jane's Addiction was as a sound and movement- insatiable, erotic rhythms, infectious guitars, G-spot bass lines, and hypnotic, narcotic vocals, all captured in perfect, sonic synchronicity by production wizard, Dave Jerden, widely considered to be the Godfather of Alternative Rock production as a result.

Perhaps rock's greatest majesty is its mystery- where do the greatest songs and sounds come from? The ones that don't try to explore, those that just do? Those that just come out of us as musicians, like the sun out of the sky, like pure inspiration. Covering the entire spectrum of human emotion by its many genres, music seeks to be the instrument of our relation to worlds within ourselves ordinarily foreign, particularly rock n' roll, which has traditionally been the most accessible and appealing- and therein, best selling - of them all. Alternative rock is definitely the most intellectual and introspective of rock n' roll's sub-genres, rooting from the place in all of us that questions. By the very nature of its sound, alternative rock is experimental, tampering with conviction and certainty, easing inhibition and exploring its roots, hedonistic, stoking erotic and exotic fires where they should not burn according to convention. Alternative rock is akin to an acid trip, the ultimate exploration of music's emotional highways and byways, boundless as the sky, deep as the ocean, and designed to force reckoning with confusion within oneself when it is by nature due to a fear of understanding. Its all about self-realization, and growth therein. The X factor in all this is *from where* that catalystic sound is created and *how* it is thereafter captured- live and in the studio. Many of rock's greatest historians feel that Jane's Addiction is the closest we've ever come to solving that sonic riddle, or at least approaching its source and soul.

Jane's Addiction's instantly-legendary catalog of albums would lay the sonic foundation for a new genre of rock- *alternative*, and a generational movement that would change the face of Rock n' Roll forever, giving way to the advent of Grunge. Speaking to a starved generation of disenfranchised listeners searching for a sonic messiah, in Perry Farrell, fans found their muse, and in his band, they discovered a sound that would prove unmatched in influence over the eruptive foundation they laid for the next popular wave of Rock n' Roll. In the course of the band's debut LP for Warner Bros., the decorously and ironically titled *Nothing's Shocking*, everything about the experience was *in fact* shocking. From the provocatively outrageous look of the band to the awesome musical vitality driving the heart of their sound, to the overwhelming impact it had upon rock's existing establishment, and beyond to the new style of music it founded- and massive sea of listeners that followed. Paralyzed by hair metal's skin-deep essence, Jane's enlightenment energized discontented rock fans to stand up and march for a cause again. The journey that followed would rock's first truly biblical one, perhaps since The Doors in the context of the hallowed weight Farrell's words carried, and how singularly and authoritatively in tune Jane's Addiction was with their time...

Perry Farrell was the first prophet in a generation, his mind a Mecca for musical meditation and discovery, his words a sanctuary for solitude and solace from the desolation of life as a teenager. What voices like John Lennon and Bob Dylan had done for their generation in the early 1960s, Farrell with Jane's Addiction would realize largely alone for his era. Kurt Cobain's popular emergence was massively catalystic for the commercial crossover of alternative rock into the sub-genre of

Grunge, but he was still as much a descendant of the sacred musical ground that Farrell had laid as Jim Morrison was of Dylan and Lennon. Intellectually, in the context of enlightenment, what had been achieved in the 1960s was truly light-years ahead of its time, the visual equivalent of the scene in *Starman* when Jeff Bridges' alien character evolves from infancy into the full maturity of manhood inside of a moment. More a spiritual adviser than a sultan, the sonic revolution Farrell and company would launch would evolve socially in that same time, causing an anonic insurrection of awareness that would inject a revitalized culture and conscience into the American mainstream as addictively as the band's very namesake. The band's sound was as cosmic as its generational appeal, running as deep as the ocean and as far as the sky, shining as brightly as the stars themselves for anyone who needed saving. Farrell gave rock n' roll back to a time of change, rather than one of derivative repetition, his band took the influences of the late 1960s and early 1970s that had become so generified and vapid in the 1980s era of style over substance, and reinvented them completely. Innovating them into something neoteric, Farrell and company gave Rock n' Roll into a new generation of social influence that could not have existed before Jane's Addiction. It was truly futuristic, giving the record industry to a commercial reformation that would be strictly adhered to, with a musically organic diet with no room for novelties, substitutes or shortcuts in the race to make a quick buck. An entire genre of rock would feed off Jane's sound, energy and fan base- as would the industry itself in the context of record sales in record time. Jane's *Addiction* was becoming Rock n' Roll's at large, and there was no denying their role as the protagonist of something powerful, ascendant, and historic in the morrow. Ear Candy Magazine noted of the band's kindred connection with their audience that "J.A. had explosive dynamism by contrasting loud and soft - violence and sensuality. The power of these themes was transferred to the audience by way of the music which was both brutal and serene."

Overnight, Jane's Addiction's impact upon popular rock was *Ocean Size*, raising a musically cultural tidal wave that crashed down upon Rock n' Roll like Judgment day, washing over the disenfranchised like a baptism, responsible for giving rise to the next pop counter-culture.

By 1987, hair metal had become an artistic insult to the artistry that had once sewn pure cantabile inspiration together with musicality, structure and innovation on a technical level, only amplified by image as a selling point, not defined by it- as bands like The Beatles and Led Zeppelin had in decades past. Over the years, the commercialization of rock wore this artistry out to the point where in its fourth generation throughout the first half of the 1980s, especially with the rise of music videos, substance was outcast permanently in favor of sales. It would take a sound so potent, so abusive of that substance that it degenerated back down to the core of what Rock n' Roll had once represented, down to the street level where the under-represented, the disenfranchised lay waiting for a rallying cry. That cry came screaming out of Hollywood's deep underground in 1988 with the major label debut of *Nothing's Shocking*. Through a brilliant blending of musical experimentation and lyrical revelation, Jane's Addiction took our disdain for how Rock n' Roll's classic derivatives were being perverted, and organized that opposition into a social explosion that would alter the genetic makeup of rock n' roll forever. Their sound was as aggressive as a riot on the rise, and revolution is exactly what it triggered. Jane's epic resonance was due in part to the fact that the band's sound encompassed so many of rock's sub-genres, fusing punk, heavy metal, prog rock, new wave, folk, and some principle elements of several others into what Rolling Stone Magazine termed to be "a huge, hybridized sound that helped define the soon-to-be-coined *alternative* (genre)...As much as any band in existence, Jane's Addiction is the true heir to Led Zeppelin, creating music that's simultaneously forbidding and weighty, delicate and ethereal. But it's never- well, hardly ever- slavishly imitative, and Jane's Addiction's version of Zeppelin is stripped of Robert Plant's fairy-tale whimsy: even when the sound is contemplative and plaintive, the sensibility is hardheaded and realistic."

Fusing boundless experimentation with hard rock convention, Jane's Addiction over the course of *'Nothing's Shocking'* and *'Ritual De La Habitual'*, produced the greatest and most influential pair of art rock albums since the two discs that comprised Pink Floyd's *The Wall*- both revitalizing and reinventing the genre in the process, inspiring the BBC to hail the latter-mentioned LPs as among "the most intense, mind-expanding albums ever heard." Now, for the first time ever, in the pages of '*Jane's Addiction: in the* Studio', fans are treated via exclusive, first-hand interviews with producer Dave Jerden, engineer Ronnie S. Champagne, who "recorded every note of" the band's classic LPs, producer Bob Ezrin, and others offering a behind-the-scenes look into the creative process of alternative rock's most provocative and ground-breaking band.

Part 2: The Birth of Jane's Addiction

With Farrell playing such a dominant direct musical impact at play within the construct of Jane's Addiction compositionally, in discovering more about the members' individual influences growing up, while Dave Navarro readily volunteered in an interview with Guitar One that, at the time, "hooking up with Perry...was really helpful to me in terms of thinking anti-guitar as much as I could while still being a guitarist. He kind of helped me listen to things a little differently." Still, delving further back into his pre-Jane's guitar heroes growing up, Navarro began by volunteering to Guitar Player that "when I was growing up, it was all about Jimi Hendrix because of his ability to perform on the neck, and all about Jimmy Page because of his studio work, his layering and texturing. When I got a little older it was all about Daniel Ash and Robert Smith, who were really effected, minimal players." Elaborating to Guitar One, Navarro added that as he progressed into his teenage years, his musical pallet expanded to include "Love and Rockets, Bauhaus, the Cure. A lot of English bands. I kind of feel like I developed a well-rounded schooling because my taste wasn't one-dimensional. I was into a lot of different types of music...As opposed to listening to one school, I listened to many schools. As a result, I was able to pick from different places and hopefully make a sound that has all of the above."

Sewing his guitar god roots as he began playing in bands, Navarro recalled in the same conversation with Guitar Player that "I also went through the phase where I was trying to learn all the Eddie stuff and all the Yngwie stuff, and I think that definitely helped my chops. But then I went through a phase where I had to try to unlearn some of it, to almost de-program myself. I got into effects a lot too, so I started toying with those, trying to find a middle ground between effected stuff and technical stuff. I don't really want to be too technical and I don't want to be too effected; even still, a lot of people would say that I am. But that combination of things is what I try to accomplish. I obviously went through that phase where I was hanging out in guitar stores. By the times Eddie was king, it was exciting for me, I had always listened to more blues-oriented rock guitarists, and the idea of guitar 'tricks' was simply fun for me. I don't think I ever put any of that type of playing into anything I did, but I certainly sat around a lot and did it. Like on '*Spanish Fly*.' He's got the pointer finger of his right hand barring behind his left hand, which is hammering. That shit was just really fun for me, but I was fortunate enough that every time I heard it coming from someone other than Van Halen, I scoffed at it. 'God, I can't believe that guy's doing that. That's Ed's thing.' But going through those years where I was playing like that helped me develop some technical finger-work."

For as much as he grew as a player during these years, Navarro shared that where composition was concerned, "I kind of remember always coming up with my own stuff, but I don't think it seriously went into practice until high school--maybe 11th grade with Steve Perkins." Meeting the drummer was a pivotal catalyst for the roots of what would eventually become the biggest alternative rock band in the world, and one the drummer himself wouldn't start out influenced by, recalling to Modern Drummer that "I grew up playing to AC/DC, and I love it. I was taught the conventional way first." Perkins' kit expanded at age 17, when he shared with Guitar Center.com that he got ahold of his first set of bongos, recalling that "from that day forward my playing changed. I sat down with the bongos at my kit and suddenly I started playing in a new way. I began playing bongo ideas on the drum set."

For bassist Eric Avery, his pre-Janes' influences, as recounted to Guitar Player Magazine, began when "I was a little stoner kid. I was into Yes and stuff like that. But by the time I got my own bass, I was into Echo and the Bunnymen and Joy Division. Our interest in the Velvet Underground and Joy Division is what initially got Perry and me together. My own bass hero is Peter Hook (of Joy Division and New Order) but I never wanted to play like him. That's the big mistake people make--mimicking their influences, instead of taking their perspective and doing something different in their own voice. That's why so many bands are cookie-mold repetitions of each other. As a band we never wanted to sound like them--we just wanted to have the same substance. Also, one of what we do is coming directly from the blues, either, thankfully enough."

For Perry, rounding out that musical collage of influences began with his sharing with journalists Al and Lawrence Livermore that "I really do love funk, more than rock. These guys like metal (Eric, David)...I'm more into black music and African music, so the contrast and variety is there. One thing we never play is blues, and that's something that Zeppelin did. Our music has a very hard vein, it's very raw rockin'. So how do you get an intelligent audience out of that? I'm really into the poetry, and the slower stuff, and I'm really into that and I don't want that end of it to drop off. That's what I think keeps this band from falling into the category of bands that can only do one thing good. It's easy to make people slam, but it's harder to make them literally enjoy slow, beautiful music. That is a higher art. And to be able to both is very rare."

Well before fate ever connected the stars that became Jane's Addiction, Perry Farrell formed the musical nucleus for what would eventually become Jane's with his mid-80s band PSI COM, whose official website offers a brief snapshot of their history as follows: "originally, a man named Rich, his wife Marisca, a man named Terry, and Duran comprised what was known as Psi Com. Being without a drummer, they placed a classified ad in the free weekly L.A. newspaper The Recycler. Farrell responded to the ad, not with the intention of becoming the group's drummer but instead as the singer. Rich agreed to let Farrell into the band as the vocalist in early '83. The ad for a drummer was left in The Recycler however, because the band was still practicing with the aid of a drum machine. Terry soon left the band and was followed closely by Rich and Marisca, who had personal differences with Farrell. Shortly after the departure of the couple, Sherer called Farrell in response to the ad for a drummer. When Sherer finally joined Duran and Farrell, the trio played their first big show, opening for The Cult at L.A.'s -Music Machine Club in the latter part of '84. When '85 hit, the group realized that they needed a bass player to fill out the bottom end of their sound. As a result, they recruited their friend Wheeler, who moved into a house with Farrell near the University of Southern California."

Bassist Kelly Wheeler offered fans an inside look at PSI COM's heyday, he began by recalling his audition for the band, explaining that "for whatever reason, the three original members of PSI COM had left, and it was Perry and two other new players- drummer Aaron Sherer and Vince Duran- and they didn't have a bass player, and had been running an ad in NOMag, which was a famous punk magazine. So I answered the ad, they called me, and we first hooked up at the house I was living in in the South Bay, and both Perry and Aaron came down for that first meeting, and just hung out and talked. I didn't know what to expect, I had never heard their stuff, even though I was aware of them. Then they said, 'Let's jam,' and we set it up to play that night at this garage they rehearsed out of off Sunset- that's how first we hooked up."

Reflecting what the bassist recalled was a powerful, contagious drive to make it among PSI COM's members, he added of the audition that "after that first jam, they called me up and said 'Yeah, we think you're great, come on board? Would you be in for it, we rehearse five days a week.' I said yes, but it was a pretty intense rehearsal schedule, which reflected I think their commitment to trying to 'make it.' Perry was very driven, no question, he was focused on that one thing, nothing else really mattered. The whole band was that way." Describing his impressions of Farrell's pre-Jane's Addiction vocal style, Wheeler first clarified that "PSI COM sounded nothing like Jane's Addiction, not even close, it was still punk. Perry had a lot of energy, but was very different from Jane's in the way he sang back then, he was really trying to mimic Joy Division more than anything. That really deep voiced, post-punk style - that was a HUGE influence for him before Jane's. Singing came very naturally to him, his chops may not have been what they are today, but his energy was just beyond anything."

Delving into the band's songwriting process, the bassist revealed that- in another departure from the way things would later be Jane's Addiction, where Farrell wrote most of the band's music- in PSI COM, "most of the music came from the band, and melodies and lyrics came from Perry, that was his thing. It always seemed like musically we were all on the same page, Perry wasn't really trying to dictate anything in PSI COM. He seemed to know what he liked when he heard something he liked, would cue in on that and really want to focus on those things. After a while, we were living in the same house together, and I would see him writing constantly in his journal- he always was writing poetry and lyrics. Sometimes his phrases didn't necessarily end up getting used in PSI COM songs, some I recognized in Jane's Addiction songs, and some he used as graphics." In what was very much an art-imitating-life approach to his rocker lifestyle, "Perry was equally as intense live as he was in rehearsal, so what people saw live is what we first saw at rehearsals, the energy was pretty much the same."

A band on the come in an underground post-punk that was beginning to burgeon in the mid-1980s, as the new line-up began playing out, bassist Kelly Wheeler recalled that "PSI COM didn't have a huge name, but were a known band at that time locally around L.A." As the band continued to build their fan base throughout L.A., Musician Magazine reported that the band experienced "a brief but exciting moment of glory in the midst of the mercurial mid-'80s Hollywood scene. The quartet played nearly as many loft parties as they did proper gigs." As Farrell shared his opinion looking back years later that of the band's contribution to the post-punk scene at the time, at the time, "we were a smash success as far as I was concerned. It wasn't a question of getting signed to a label, because that wasn't even a possibility in those days. What was important was that we were recognized among our peers. I saw our name in the LA Weekly as one 'one of the best new bands in the city,' and I was completely thrilled. I'd tune in the college radio stations just to hear our name get mentioned in the club listings. And, playing at the Anti-Club..." Drummer Aaron Sherer added of the band's place among their live-scene that "we dovetailed perfectly for a while in terms of philosophy, creativity and music. Nothing too mystical, but the parts added up to something bigger, which is exactly what the people are after when they play in bands."

Feeling after a short while that they needed to put some of the magic they were creating live down on tape, bassist Kelly Wheeler shared his recollection that "the demo was something we knew we needed to do, but it took a while to come together. At first, we just played live and rehearsed our asses off, then when we saw an opportunity at Radio Tokyo, we all kicked in equally on the studio time and made it happen. We hadn't done any demoing before then, we'd just fleshed the songs out between rehearsals and live dates, so we were well prepared. We had a ten to twelve song live set, but we focused on what we felt were the five strongest songs for the demo." According to the band's Myspace.com biography, "in March of '85, Psi Com made plans to release a five-song, 12-inch EP. The band entered Radio Tokyo Studios in Venice, CA that spring and cut the songs *'Xiola,' 'Human Condition,' 'Ho Ka Hey,' 'Words'* and *'City of Nine Gates.'* Ethan James manned the boards for the sessions, which lasted for one weekend. James was known for producing seminal punk group the Minutemen's most popular album *'Double Nickels on the Dime.'* " Farrell recalled of the band's demo sessions that "it was funny, because our engineer was also making soundtracks for dirty movies in his back room: Johnny Deep or something. It was kind of creepy to see him sitting at the board with this strange smile on his face."

Detailing the band's routine during recording, bassist Kelly Wheeler recalled that "we didn't usually start tracking till after 6, and would go till sometimes till 3 or 4 in the morning, it was just whole nights. We did multiple takes of songs, and punches, repairs for guitar and bass overdubs. We tracked live off the floor, and the basic tracks were kept. Perry did scratch vocal tracks with us, and then did his vocal and percussion tracks as overdubs afterward." Musician Magazine offered a further elaboration on the band's gear list utilized in the course of recording the demo, offering that "on their EP, Aaron Sherer bashed away at a six-piece set of DW drums. Bassist Kelly Wheeler used the full-scale, small-bodied Ibanez bass the band bought for him when he became a member, and ran it through an SWR bass amp. Vince Duran ran his late-'70s Fender Start through a 50-watt Music Man and a Roland JC 120 Jazz Chorus. His specialty at the time was bending his whammy bar 'the wrong way' to achieve various warbling effects. Farrell contributed percussion as well as vocals to the record, applying sticks to church bells, hubcaps and a Chevy engine block."

Once Perry had turned his attention to tracking the album's proper lead vocals, in the same conversation with Musician Magazine, he recalled of his signature use of multi-layered effects in the studio that it began and ended with "the Ibanez EM-1000 echo unit...(was what) I had back then. You get a much wilder effect spinning the knobs on that unit than you do pushing buttons on anything digital. If you want to sound like me when you sing, you need to find a beat-up, 10-year-old analog echo effect." Indeed, bassist Kelly Wheeler added that "Perry's signature Yamaha delay, I would say that was utilized even more so back in PSI COM actually than Jane's, he used that thing on the record as well as in rehearsals and live.

Of the five songs the band tracked during the Radio Tokyo session, Musician would identified 'Xiola' as "a moment of epiphany in (Farrell's) vocal development," a song where bassist Kelly Wheeler agreed "Perry sort of broke out in Xiola, that was one of the key songs that gave a clue to his new direction." Farrell later added in an interview with the same publication that "I'd never really sung the way I did on that one before. I thought that, for the sake of the recorded version, I'd scream as loud and hard as I could. I started screeching on some high notes, and that's where you can actually hear my real voice being born." Completed just prior to the summer of 1985, the band's official Myspace bio recalled that "in July, PSI COM had 1,500 copies of their self-titled EP produced to release on their own label, Mohini. When the records were delivered from the pressing plant, the band was in shock, as more than half of the EPs were warped."

In spite of the debacle with the E.P.'s pressing, by the fall of 1985, the band had reached what bassist Kelly Wheeler and other group members remembered as the peak of their popularity, beginning with the bassist's recollection that "by the fall of that year, we were drawing 100 people a show after the EP came out, and starting to play bigger venues. We toured that fall with Camper Van Beethoven, and some other really cool bands." The band would break up later in the fall of that same year, with Perry Farrell offering to Musician Magazine his closing observation that "the end of our chapter was right around the end of the scene we were part of. Shortly after we broke up, D. Boon died, Savage Republic broke up, and Patrick Mata went over to England and broke up Kommunity FK. TSOL started dressing up. A year later, Guns N' Roses were everywhere, and it was cool to pay-to-play in the clubs. Penelope Spheeris started teasing her hair, and it was all over." While artists of a lesser vision might have- and in many later famous cases- try to change their style up to adapt to the changing rock scene, Perry Farrell took it upon himself to design his own rock sub-genre within the musical construct of what would soon become Jane's Addiction, in the process changing the course of alternative rock forever.

The first member of Jane's Addiction to hook up with Perry Farrell was bassist Eric Avery, who recalled that he'd first seen the band live before ever hooking up with Farrell, sharing with Details Magazine that "(my girlfriend) Carla asked me if I'd seen Psi Com and I said, 'Yeah, I think they blow.' And she went, 'Oh, okay,' and tried to move on to the next topic. So I said, 'Why are you asking me?' 'Well, they're looking for a bass player, but it doesn't matter.' It was such a pivotal moment that could so easily have gone another way." When Avery finally agreed to an audition to replace Wheeler, Farrell recalled in an interview with the same publication feeling instantly that "Eric was a hell of a bass player. I asked him to join Psi Com." Sharing his initial impression of Perry as one where the singer was "just a really charming, dynamic, crazy person," the bassist seemed more immediately excited about the fact that "our musical tastes were almost identical." Keeping to a stripped-down early sound that Farrell was integral to the band's sound as it developed, future guitarist Dave Navarro would explain years later of Farrell's philosophy that "I would say that my biggest musical influence is Perry...He was someone with the skills, talent, creativity and artistic vision to help me trim the fat off my playing." Avery recalled at the time that the group's initial sound was so stripped down that "we went into this like a pair of art-damaged kids. I remember playing to try to get a grant from this art school downtown. I just played on these chemical drums, and he sang."

Re-naming the band Jane's Addiction, Perry would recall his impetus for the group name coming from his rationale "when I first named the band, (that) I use the name Jane rather than, say, John, because it was a very anti-macho thing to do, like calling yourself Sue (or Alice!). We weren't afraid to play softly, with tenderness, which is a word men tend to cringe over." When the pair decided to expand their player's club to include a guitarist and drummer, Steve Perkins shard with Details Magazine that he joined the band simply through the fact that "they were auditioning drummers and I got the chance." As for future guitarist Dave Navarro, he recalled in an interview with Guitar World that "(it was) very incestuous. Stephen had hooked up with Perry through Eric Avery, the bass player. Stephen was dating Eric's sister, Rebecca, who was my ex-girlfriend. I had introduced Stephen to her. Eric asked Stephen to play in Jane's Addiction. They needed a guitar player and Stephen said, 'My friend Dave's really great.' He called me up and asked me if I'd be into it. I said, Sure."

Sharing with Details that "I had actually seen Jane's Addiction play before. They were great," when the band first got together to jam, Navarro added in an interview with Guitar Player his feeling looking back years later that "it was four different guys who really, honestly had no business being together. Eric hated Led Zeppelin. I loved Led Zeppelin. So I'd bring in a Led Zeppelin vibe in my playing and he would bring a Joy Division vibe in his playing. Which was much better than if we were both coming from the same place. Then we just would have been a bad version of Led Zeppelin, or of Joy Division." Taking advantage of that eclectic and at times contrary melting pot of musical influences, band leader Perry Farrell from the start sought to capitalize on the players differences to build a unique unison that he explained to a rock journalist led to "eighty percent of our material (thriving on tension)...Putting together elements that might not seem to fit."

Though he would have a heavy hand in the compositional and production side of the band's sound as time went on, in their early days, Farrell sought to keep the band as free to focus on experimentation as possible, reasoning to one journalist at the time that "what (we play is)...freestyle, with everybody going for what they wanted. It didn't seem that there were any limitations for what the wanted. It didn't seem that there were any limitations for what anybody was doing. There wasn't a formula like, 'Okay, this is for four measures, this is for eight.' It was just like, 'Go for it, let's feel it out." Indeed, as drummer Steven Perkins recalled in an interview with Modern Drummer the rhythm of the band's early rehearsals, "we were all just so young when Jane's started, and, as for the music, it was 'three...four...crash!' Everything would be a blow-up , all you could put into it."

Of colossal importance in the collaborative chemistry between guitarist Dave Navarro and singer Perry Farrell in the band's early days was their mutual love of delay, which Navarro recalled to Boss.com was the buckle of their musical bond given "Perry and I are from different musical backgrounds. Back then he was coming from more of a goth-band situation, and he was playing with vocal delays in that band, called PsiCOM. I was coming from a band called Disaster with Stephen Perkins, which was more of a speed-metal band. I was heavily influenced by David Murray of Iron Maiden at the time. That song '*The Ides of March*' off the Killers album has a musical intro with lots of delay on the guitar. As soon as I heard that... I loved that sound. So Perry and I were both experimenting with delays at different points in our creative pasts, and when we met, the only thing we had in common musically was our love of delay. Which was interesting, in terms of making the Jane's sound happen, 'cause it was a combination of him coming from where he was coming from and me coming from where I was coming from, being totally different musical places."

One musical arena where the young guitarist was willing to defer to Farrell's influence came with lessons in letting go, explaining to Guitar World that "Perry is the kind of guy who moves through things really quickly. He gets really into something and then kind of moves beyond it. And because of that, he's always into something new. And he brings in elements of all those things, whether it be ethnic music or whatever. When Jane's Addiction started, Perry was really into reggae, which Eric and I both hated. But the elements of reggae that Perry brought into Jane's Addiction were ideas of dub and so forth. And he was really into non-traditional rock instrumentation...What was funny about that blues thing was, when I first joined the band, the guys in Fishbone were throwing all these tapes to Perry. 'Check this out; check that out.' And they were all blues guitar, like B.B. King. Things I couldn't imagine even listening to back then. And Perry would say, 'Listen to how simply he's playing that riff.' So I took those tapes home and started playing; and I said, 'Yeah, I kinda got this blues thing down.' And then Perry told me to forget everything he'd told me! It would always be like that. On one hand, it made things very confusing for me, as a player. But the bright side was that it pushed me, at least at that age--I was 18, 19 years old--to do the same thing he was doing, which was getting into specific types of music, learning about them, mastering them to a certain degree and then scrapping them...When I hooked up with Jane's Addiction, I was a kid--very impressionable. I had strong opinions about what music should be. Playing with them contributed to that in a very broad way. It opened my eyes to a whole lot of different possibilities as to what music is about."

That eternal sense of open-mindedness where the band's ever-evolving sound was concerned allowed them to represent something on the Sunset Strip that at the time no other rock, metal or alt-rock band was offering audiences- a sound that, for Farrell, reflected a "taste (that) goes from funk, hip hop, reggae, anything that's really bassy." With their own sub-genre of rock to offer music fans craving an alternative to the hair-metal heavy Sunset Strip club scene, drummer Steven Perkins recalled in an interview with Ink 19 that "we had a moment in 1986 when things were ready for a change and -- you know what? -- we were happy to do it. Not only were we putting on our own shows and staying away from the typical Sunset Strip clubs, we were also throwing our own parties in downtown LA that didn't start until one or two in the morning. The band was just part of the party, it wasn't like just going to a club to see a band; we had a nice little scene happening. That scene allowed us to explore musically. David and I were just eighteen when Jane's started. Perry was twenty-six and Eric was twenty-three or twenty-four. They were into different types of music and they were out of high school for years, while Dave and I had just graduated. We were into more of a hard rock, Led Zeppelin-heavy sound, and we had been playing that type of stuff in our high school years. Then Dave and I met those cats, they were more into Echo & The Bunnymen, Joy Division, Siouxsie & the Banshees and Bauhaus. I think that was the sound of Jane's Addiction; mine and David's electronic craziness -- you know, we loved to do little flurries, fast drum fills and guitar fills -- and Eric and Perry's slow, deep, dark sound. At that moment, the scene had, in LA at least, a lot of the glam rock with Ratt and Motley Crue and other bands that sounded like them. Many of the people I knew were not going for that, for whatever reason. Then, all of a sudden, there was a big scene that happened and there it was; Jane's Addiction had the chance to lead it. We took it seriously, too."

So too did local rock critics and A&R executives hungry for any band that could entertain so many varying fan bases in one time. Quickly, the band entered Radio Tokyo Studios in Venice, California to record what would become their first real demo, co-produced by Perry Farrell and engineer Ethan James, and consisting of *'Jane Says,' 'Pigs In Zen,' 'Mountain Song,' 'Had A Dad,'* and *'I Would For You.'* Soon thereafter, the band signed a management deal with XXX Records, which released the band's first official LP, the now-classic *'XXX Live'*, recorded live at the Roxy Theatre for a meager $4000.00 on January 26th, 1987. Billboard Magazine's review of the album years later would note that, at the time, "the L.A. band's unorthodox fusion of Led Zeppelin-influenced hard rock, dark Velvet Underground-ish imagery, and stream-of-consciousness art rock wasn't as focused or confident as it would be on the commanding *Ritual de lo Habitual*. But even so, the band showed considerable potential."

As Rolling Stone Magazine next reported- "after releasing a self-titled live album on L.A.'s Triple X Records in 1987, a major-label bidding war ensued," with the Dallas Morning News adding ahead of the band's getting signed that "(Jane's Addiction are) the first runners-up to Guns N' Roses as Los Angeles' most hyped musical eminence." As engineer Ronnie Champagne- who sat side by side with the band throughout the complete recordings of both *'Nothing's Shocking'* and *'Ritual De Lo Habitual'* - recalled at the outset of their collaboration, "Jane's got signed because of their buzz. They created the buzz before they got signed, it wasn't an invention; it wasn't just a band with a whole bunch of development money thrown at them. The band's sound and image were already intact."

That sense of artistic integrity and freedom was rooted at the core of the band's sound and scene, and at the top of their demands when negotiating with the countless A&R heads lined up around the block of major labels courting Jane's Addiction heading into the late spring of 1987. As Perry Farrell confirmed to rock journalists Al and Lawrence Livermore at the time the band was being shopped to majors, "we did have all these record labels coming at us, but my artistic integrity and the whole band's artistic integrity comes first. And as far as popularity it can become contrary because I get nervous sometimes because of the popularity, but it is popular and I'm not going to slow down. I've never gone to be a commercial guy, and never have gone out to try to get the record companies to fall in love with us." Elaborating, guitarist Dave Navarro in an interview with Guitar Player recalled that the band indeed took advantage of holding the cards they did as a negotiating tactic, recalling that "(the labels) all pretty much wanted us. Other labels offered us more money than Warner Bros, but we went with them because they were willing to let us do what we wanted, production-wise, with the artwork, videos...everything. We just did what we wanted to do, regardless of what anyone told us. When we signed with Warner Bros. we kept all creative control. That's so important when you sign!"

"There's been alot of importance put on the two Jane's Addiction albums I did with them." - Dave Jerden

"The most important thing a label has to understand is that we want to go against the grain of what's being done. Nothing new is going to come out if you don't try to change (what's already been done)." - Perry Farrell, 1987

Chapter 3
Nothing's Shocking

In Rock n' Roll's greater universe, Jane's Addiction historically is a giant, psychedelic, and organic musical planet that has held its own against derivative musical moons which circled within its gravitational pull- moons attracted primally to the creative maternity that made Jane's star innately shine the brightest. In metaphorical context of the earth's solar system, Jane's Addiction is arguably most kindred to Jupiter, traditionally considered one of the more dominant planets within our solar system, with multi-colored rings that continuously alter in color and morphology. With an animate sound that continually changes moods and energies while preserving musical consonance, Jane's importance in terms of maintaining the historical order of the various sub-genres' solar system within Rock's larger cosmoses cannot be understated.

Like the aforementioned planet, the band's sound and influence will be studied for generations to come. Rolling Stone Magazine's review of the band's debut album, *Nothing's Shocking*, produced by Dave Jerden, hailed both the band and their musical epic as "the latest great hope of the Los Angeles club scene, a product of a city whose often overlooked hard-rock scene has long been every bit as successful and commercially productive as its more heralded punk and post punk scene...Jane's Addiction, young and restless, makes music that scrapes against the smooth surfaces of commercial pop. But this perverse, willful, Los Angeles-bred artist...straddles the line between the two camps, and several others: the band is indulgent and excessive, adept at typically screeching (but atypically original) hard-rock guitar raveups and at flights into dreamy psychedelia. A classic *love 'em or hate 'em* outfit, the band is great, and it is also full of shit – often at the same time, a dichotomy that may be the edge that sustains *Nothing's Shocking*. (The songs) are hard-boiled riff rockers, unsettling, lyrically incisive and musically excessive. Best of all is *Jane Says*...from the strummed acoustic guitar that carries it along to the song's acid-etched portrait of an addict, the song is a worthy Left Coast successor to *Walk on the Wild Side*."

Journeying back to the first time he physically entered the world that was Jane's Addiction, producer Dave Jerden recalled that "when I met with the band, the first rehearsal we met together, I said 'How I see this is theatre. Its going to be a dramatic production, and what I want to do is consider having acts, like there's an opening crescendo, which is '*Up the Beach*', and what I want to do is plan the record as far as what songs are going to go in what order', and we rehearsed the songs in that order, and recorded them in that order. And we kept everything, in terms of a theatrical, dramatic play. And that was my idea, was that it was going to be, the curtain opens, and the fanfare of the orchestra, and then you go to this trip with Jane's Addiction, and the trip you're going on, what its about, is an exploration of our culture. Its an exploration of all the things that are happening. There were alot of things that were starting to happen at that time with computers, and the internet was in its infancy, the pace was quickening with technology within our society. There was lots of stuff going on, and Jane's Addiction to me was like Jimi Hendrix- who was perfect for his time, his guitar sounded like explosions, Viet Nam was going on at that time, he had an international sound, we were becoming a global community at that time, and Jimi Hendrix captured in sound the feel of society at that time. And for me, Jane's Addiction is the same thing. I once saw them play at Scream, at 3 o'clock in the morning, and there were like 3,000 kids waiting in line to get in, and what they played was like an old theatre, and the show was very theatrical and dramatic, and this was before we started the record, and was where I got the idea of the record being a dramatic play. The over-all feel of that record to me was that it should reflect the culture- be chaotic, and makes sense at some times, and at others, doesn't make any sense at all. Just constant stimula coming at you from all different angles, as the culture was doing. And that's what I wanted to capture on the record. They're a band for the future, that's the kind of band they are at heart."

With Rolling Stone Magazine quipping that Farrell was "reputedly a control freak" in the band's early days, drummer Steven Perkins recalled in a label press release that, initially, "Warners was trying to find a producer for us on the first record, but we said, 'No, we want produce it ourselves, at least co-produce it.' So they agreed to put us into a studio and let us produce a track ourselves. We did this cool sounding version of 'Ocean Size' and when Warners heard it, they gave us the thumbs up to CO-produce the next record." Settling quickly on Dave Jerden, the producer recalled responding immediately to the organized chaos contained within Jane's Addiction's singular sound, sharing that "truthfully, at that time, I was going through alot of personal problems, my marriage was breaking up, my father was dying- and I just said 'Fuck it' on that record, I don't care what's happening on the radio, I'm just going to do whatever I want, and that was Perry's contribution to the whole record, he said 'Let's just do whatever we want- fuck everything!' " That bravery played an central role in translating Jane's

Addiction's musical evolution in the studio into the cultural revolution it became in the early 1990s- embraced by what many consider to be rock's last great generation of bands.

Continuing, the producer added his memory that "when they were getting signed, they talked to alot of producers, and every producer wanted to change them. Perry told me this one producer said 'If we do this, this, and this, I can make you sound like U2.' And another famous producer wanted to fire Perry and get a new singer. And when he came and met with me, it was really low key. He brought the whole band down, and said 'Is there is something you can play me?' And I was sitting in this office across the hallway from the studio, and it was just a mess, and there was an old acetate laying there of a band I'd worked with, that had a bunch of percussion on it, so I said 'I might as well play this.' And Perry said what sold him on me was my nonchalance, non-intense like 'I gotta have this gig!' I was low key, just like 'This is what I do, and if you like it, great, if you don't like it, I understand. Good luck.' "

It was understood between all parties heading into pre-production that the buck stopped with Perry Farrell, which according to engineer Ronnie Champagne required "the members of the band- to be successful on that record- they each had to suspend their own individual creativity a bit to accommodate Perry's vision, and Perry didn't have to because it was HIS record deal. Perry owned the name to the band, had gotten the deal with Warners', and he knew what he wanted and knew that if he was allowed to make the record he heard in his head, it would be a sound the world had never heard before." In some ways, the band seemed agreeable to the latter arrangement, with guitarist Dave Navarro sharing with journalist Malcolm Dome that while at the time he didn't "know what his overall vision" was, he trusted implicitly enough in Farrell's artistic vision that he "could hate everything he says and still stay in this band." Musically, the guitarist added to Details Magazine that, at the time, "when Perry sang, I got the chills. There's something about playing with him that's magical. It's like playing with nobody else in the world."

As the songs for 'Nothing's Shocking' came together, drummer

Steve Perkins shared his memory with a rock journalist that "the original songs were written in the house on Wilton. I remember showing up when everyone got off work, going into the garage, and writing all those songs-- *'Whores,' 'Pigs in Zen.'* It's like that moment you fall in love." While the band may have been in love with their creative process ahead of entering the studio, which was also preceded by what engineer Ronnie Champagne recalled as a series of "pre-production rounds was sat down and figured out all the parts we felt were necessary for that track, then we'd make a chalk-board list for each track, and just mark things off until we were done."

As well as things were going for the band heading into production, producer Dave Jerden recalled to Details Magazine that "it started out with lots of enthusiasm because it was their first major-label album. Then three weeks into it a definite pall came over things. Perry said he had been talking to an attorney." Farrell's reason for hiring an attorney was in response to what he recalled as the band's desire to "split the publishing evenly, which is fine if the songwriting is evenly, but it was my work. Songwriting isn't something something to carve up democratically. There's an art to it, and it takes a lot of time, even when it looks simpler." Adding that "one guy brought in his dad's lawyer to represent the three of them...when we had our own lawyer", the singer conceded that "that caused a tremendous division."

For as unhappy as the band might have been with Farrell's proposed royalty structure, engineer Ronnie Champagne pointed out that "another reason why Perry has co-production credits on those records: its because he wrote all those songs, EVERY part. He taught Dave Navarro what to play for guitar solos, sat there, recited and banged the parts out to Dave, it was very physical. Perry's a very physical person, and he would sit there with his body and show him the feeling and accents of the solos, work out drum patterns with Steven, etc." Qualifying the latter, drummer Steven Perkins offered to Drum World years later that "Perry's a great drummer. Technically, he can't shred, but he can get back there and think of some crazy beat that you or I would never think of. A lot of people don't realize that Stevie Wonder played drums on a lot of his old records, and he came up with some groovy beats. The guy's a keyboard player, he wasn't taught kick/snare, he was just taught music." Still, bassist Eric Avery recalled in an interview with Guitar Player that, at the time, from the band's vantage point, when "we started talking about publishing splits and that did not go well. The seed of resentment was planted there. We actually broke up for a couple of days."

Once the band had worked out their differences and production got underway, engineer Ronnie Champagne shared his memory that "*Nothing's Shocking* was a long record to record, easily 6-8 weeks, maybe a bit longer. I recorded every noise made on that record. I was working so hard on it that if it had been 6 months, I wouldn't have noticed. I don't remember anything about my personal life during that period, not one fucking thing." As the album took shape, Perry's commitment to his sonic vision was indeed reflected in the hours the band spent in the studio bringing the record Farrell heard in his head to life. Offering Melody Maker a glimpse inside just how much blood, sweat and tears he and his band had invested in seeing that sound through, he reasoned that "as far as doing something great and epic, I'm all for it, I'll do whatever I have to to create something like that. Great bands and great music are too few and far between."

From he and Jerden's vantage point, engineer Ronnie Champagne recalled that, in the interest of accommodating Farrell's musical vision, "with Jane's, everything was bigger than life, that was the goal: 'We're going to make this huge.' And from the gate, it had to be huge sounding. That was always the consideration. It wasn't really requested of me as an engineer to do that, it was just understood that this is going to be really big in all senses of the word. It wasn't like we were trying to do anything different than anyone else has done since Led Zeppelin, but we were trying to capture as much of that style as possible." In terms of substance, Perry explained to Melody Maker that with Nothing's Shocking, he was seeking to "try to make the band as well-rounded and as much sex and violence as there is, there's also love and tenderness and happiness...There's funny things and sad things, it should be like a movie." That is precisely how fans and critics alike would eventually receive the album, as reflected in Rolling Stone Magazine's observation that "one of the funniest things about *Nothing's Shocking*, Jane's Addiction's much-ballyhooed 1988 release, was how it skewed the conventions of L.A. Sunset Strip metal, managing to be distinctively perverse in a world already saturated with bad taste and bacchanalia. At times the music was glorious, playful psychedelic metal, as Perry Farrell's avant-gypsy garb, weird eye makeup and prepubescent voice plugged you into the visionary amorality of children. With its trippy nature imagery and porno bent, *Nothing's Shocking* struck the gong."

Back in the studio, with recording underway, engineer Ronnie Champagne's attentions in the early weeks of tracking were primarily focused on capturing the band's thunderous drum sound, with the engineer explaining that "the challenge with Steve's kit at that time is that he didn't really have a great drum set. He had a good drum set, but nothing like his DW kit on Ritual. It was a Ludwig set with a whole bunch of drums with only one skin on them on the tops, and I think I used about every microphone in the house recording that kit because we recorded top and bottom. If you use a good studio drum set, you only need to record the top heads because the drums sing, but in a case where you have no heads on the bottom, the drum doesn't have much of a tone- except on the top it sounds like a whack with no tone. So we put mics on the bottoms of the tom, and basically the toms were really muted. We put 57s on the top and bottom on the snare, and the kick had a Senheisser D-12, in combination with another close mic, usually an RE-20. I've found typically, just off of the floor, like the U-47 tube mic out in front of the drums 12 feet or so away, just to get that low end of the kick drum. For the close-micing, we used up as many dynamic mics as we had, being 421s or 57s or RE-20s Obviously, the smaller the drum, the smaller the diaphragm of the microphone that we used. So the smaller toms had 57s and the bigger toms had 421s, so the capsule of the mic got bigger as the drum got bigger. Through the rack- and I remember it was an expensive rack of toms he had- so I top and bottom-miced, usually a combination of 421s and 57s, a 57 on the top, and 421 on the bottom."

Describing the dynamics of the room itself he and Jerden had Perkins set up in, the engineer added that "when it came to overheads, we actually did the room and overheads first, where I had the drums set up in the room, then threw up a pair of overhead mics, threw up a pair of room mics, and threw up a pair of center mics when capturing close to the drums and far away from the drums. It was a pretty large, bright room with a glass wall on one side and cement on the other, and then drywall on the others. SO when you hit something in there, it bounced around like crazy. It was a rectangular room, and if you were looking from the glass toward the end of the room where the drummer would be sitting on a stool, the right hand side of the room was cut off in a corner because we had put some ISO-booths in there. That sort of chopped-up all the parallel walls, but didn't really, because it was still a really loud, bright room. So using a pair of C-12s about 2/3rds of the way back in the room from the drummer, up into the room with the standard studio boom microphone stands, the big ones that go up like 25 feet. I set those up about 12 feet in the air with the mics pointed down diagonally at the center of the drum kit, from the extreme left and right. I believe there was also a C-24 in the middle of the room, maybe not quite 2/3rds back from the kick, placed six feet up- and that was the triangle."

Elaborating on the sonic challenges he faced in the course of micing such a grand room, Champagne explained that "in a room that size, the tone of the individual drums occasionally gets drowned out by the brashy, thrashiness of the cymbals, especially with that kind of kit and that kind of playing. So at that point its about pointing the diaphragms and using your headphones out in the room so that you're not getting all the brashness of the cymbals. You're trying to point the diaphragms of the microphones under the cymbals so that the cymbals will be picked up using another pair of mics, or even another two pairs of mics as overheads. We used 451s and 452s for overheads, and then on top of that, the big trick of the day was using a Senheisser shotgun mic way above the drummer's head, pointed right down at the top of the snare drum to give you that smack... that smack with wood, we liked to call it. Because when you top and bottom mic the snare drum, you're getting a really hard hit off the 57 on the top, and a really kind of fuzzy, stringer sound from the bottom of the snare that you kind of blend in delicately just enough. Its more air than anything else. When you take it away, you know that its missing, but when its in there, it just has to be in there a little bit for me to have this 3-dimensional sound, and the shotgun mic really booms back how the snare impact sounds in the whole room. Because you're getting 10 feet between the impact and the diaphragm of the microphone, which means there's a lot of air moving in there. And during that time- which is milliseconds- you actually capture some width. It doesn't give you any width in the stereo element, but you hear it sonically. So because the room was so brash and loud with so many hard surfaces, I used a C-24 wearing headphones to walk around and find the center of the room. There's a brashness and a warmth going hard- the brashness is coming from all the brass of the cymbals, and the warmth is coming from the air that the drums move, and you're trying to find a spot in the middle where its warmer than brassy, and that's your center spot. So now when I'm at the console listening to it, I can get my sense of depth between the 3 mics that are trying to pick up the room. And that's just to avoid phase cancelling, so you're trying to use the room where it sounds the nicest."

One area Perkins himself was a sticklar about during tracking was tuning, sharing with Modern Drummer that, in the studio, "I'm very much into tuning my drums correctly and getting a good sound straight from that and going with it. Engineers usually hate me because I don't put anything in my kick drum, just the two heads. It's loud, but if you tune the heads right, it only rings as much as a floor tom would. When I bought my first drumset, all it came with was the two heads and a felt strip, so I learned to tune it like that. An engineer might want me to at least put a pillow in there, but then you have these nice, resonant toms and a 'thud' for a kick. Then the biggest drum is the softest instrument. It doesn't make any sense. I'll tell an engineer, 'Why don't you just put a microphone in front of the head, let me tune it, and if it sounds good on stage, but not in the speakers, tell me what you need me to do--whether it's too ringy, too dead--and I'll tune it.' That, to me, is the way you should make music. But you get to the point where engineers say, 'We could use an electronic kit and it'll sound just as good, Steve. We could plug it in--no tuning.' But that hurts me. I feel like the drum is there for a drum reason. If you know how to tune a floor tom or kick drum, tune it. People are taping and muffling because they can't get the overtones out of drums. But you're the drummer, you should know what you want to hear, so learn how to tune your drums. I'll spend an hour, sweating, frustrated over it, only to find out one of the heads is busted, but I'll just get a new head and work it out. And I never like the feel of hitting a drum with something in it, like there's something in the way."

As Perkins laid his drum tracks, Farrell sat side by side with engineer Champagne and producer Jerden in the control room, though- as the engineer recalled- "the only time Perry really made percussion suggestions was if something was missing he thought should be there. He was very descriptive in his language, and there was a mystic element to the way he produced. He would sound out percussive ideas he had, a flanger for instance, so he very much knew in his head what sound he wanted and that's how he got it out to the rest of the band as the record was made. He did a lot of producing with his mouth, quite literally." One area where Champagne recalled he and Perkins "pretty much had free reign" came "when it came time to play percussion and do overdubs, that's when me and Steve had the most fun. The rhythm parts in that sense were pretty much me and Steve- and he's awesome." Perkins added to Modern Drummer that "as a drummer, I always thought it wasn't about how fast you can do a double-stroke roll; it's about rhythms and melodies. Listening to the bongos and letting them lead the way rhythmically on my drum set opened up my mind; I found that I could replicate the rhythms on the kit."

When attentions turned to tracking bassist Eric Avery, engineer Ronnie Champagne began by recalling that "on Eric's bass, I used an RE-20 and 57 mic combo during recording," while the bassist added in an interview with Guitar Player that when composing his bass parts, "my lines start out with what comes naturally, then I strip away whatever I can, trying to do something interesting. I think 'uncomplicated' and 'interesting' are almost invariably synonymous." Offering '*Whores*' as an example, the bassist adds that "the bass line stays in B the entire time; we just used dynamics to make the verse different from the chorus. It's more of a primitive thing. No, that's too pretentious--more of a *core* thing. I don't really listen with my left brain. I have to play a line over and over exactly the same way for a good ten minutes before I can decide whether I like it. I'm looking for a feeling rather than a sound." Detailing his gear to the same journalist, Avery recalled that "I got my first bass when I was 17, the Fender Precision I play today. I just can't play any other. I've had endorsement offers, but I can't part with it--it's like a teddy bear attachment. I have a backup Precision, but I only use it in times of dire emergency. I used a Trace-Elliot amp for a long time. I got a great sound, but the amp was just too delicate."

For guitarist Dave Navarro, his creative nature mirrored that of Farrell's in context of visualization, explaining to journalist Dave Thompson that "when I hear music, I see colors, and I think we're a real colorful band, even though there aren't a lot of instruments." Acknowledging Farrell's heavy influence at play throughout the course of tracking the guitars for Nothing Shocking, Navarro reasoned in an interview with Guitar World that "(Perry) brought his creative force to our playing, honing it into something a little bit more accessible in terms of other people being able to understand it. The best example I could give you is maybe I'd be playing a guitar part that was from Pluto and Perry would say, 'That sounds great, but make it from Neptune.' " One area the pair shared a common love for- that of experimentation- was of a great aid as they navigated their way through the psychedelic layers of guitar soundscape that decorated the record, sharing with Boss.com his memory that "effect wise, (Perry and I) were pretty much on the same page," adding in an interview with Guitar World that "I love echo--its the greatest mask a guitar player can have...It can makes something boring really interesting, and it can cover up a lot of shit. Perry uses a lot of echo on his vocals, too. It adds tension."

Elaborating on the technique he applied in the course of painting the band's songs with effect accents as original as the sound itself the band was bringing to life, Navarro explained to Guitar One that "I guess like the droning with the delay; the wetness. I don't know, to me that's a sound that is just comfortable. That sound helps take me to another place, and that's what I want playing music to do for me. Considering the fact that I'm not a big drug user anymore, I don't have very many things to take me to other places other than music or sex or whatever devices I can find. I think the effects thing started off when I joined Jane's Addiction. Perry and I were both really into delay, and for me, I felt that when I would go into a guitar solo or something would drop out because

I was the only guitarist. So I always found that if I stepped on a delay: a) the mistakes I made were undetectable; and b) it seemed to be fuller sounding. That just kind of stuck with me and became a thing that I enjoy."

Adding the technical commentary concerning Navarro's pedals, engineer Ronnie Champagne recalled that the guitarist favored the "Ibanez delay- there's only a couple sounds that box makes, which is either an up or down modulation in the feedback of the delay itself, or the opposite. So Dave would step on his wawa, hit the delay at the same time, so he could make some sort of a screeching noise, then grab the feedback knob and actually turn it, and he had foot switches to turn off the echo while he was still playing. Dave had a lot of rhythmic parts being played into the echo itself." Navarro, for his own part, explained in a conversation with Guitar World that in addition to the Ibanez delay, he also used "a regular Boss digital delay, and the repeats are set so that they go forever. You can set the delay time three different ways, and then there's another knob that controls the speed of that particular position. I'll turn the position knob and the speed knob," adding to Boss.com of his love affair with the pedal that it in fact dated back to childhood, such that "I've been playing BOSS pedals since I was a kid. My first BOSS pedal was the T-Wah (TW-1). God, I must have been 12 or 13 at the time. Then I got myself a little flanger, got myself one of those orange distortion pedals (DS-1), some delays (DD-series), and pretty much haven't been using anything else since. There was a time during the '80s when all the guitarists were using these rackmount rigs, and I swapped over for about a minute. I tried to dial up different tones and effects with all the rackmount stuff, but I realized that it took away the ability to turn knobs on the floor the way I liked, so I scrapped it and went back to the BOSS stuff."

Engineer Champagne offered his additional recollection on the way the sound was brought to life that during the album's subsequent mixing sessions, "the way we mixed those guitars, you're not necessarily hearing all of those guitars at any one time, its like gears in a car when you're driving. Jerry Cantrell was the first to explain it that way, but for Jane's it was very much that way, where each guitar part was a gear change, and with a band as dynamic as Jane's Addiction was as far as the tonal interchanges going on, that were often times psychedelic, and sweet and beautiful. With that band, especially with Perry and Steven, who is a deadhead and had a CLOSET FULL of Grateful Dead live concerts on tape, there's a certain Grateful Dead influence at work there. They all brought that psychedelic influence to play, including Dave."

As he laid his stacks of rhythm guitar tracks, Navarro offered to Guitar World a glimpse inside his recording process where the guitarist explained "I like to fill up as many tracks as are available with guitar ideas. Usually, when I go into the studio, I don't necessarily know what it is I'm going to try and accomplish. It usually ends up taking on its own life. Then I step back and delete tracks or combine tracks and see what kind of tapestry can be woven. I prefer that to going into the studio with a concrete idea and then trying to accomplish that, because I've found that if I have a concrete idea of what I want, I usually can't get it." From behind the console, engineer Ronnie Champagne recalled that "as Dave was tracking guitars, typically what we would do is record rhythm guitars for the main track- which could be as little as two, or as many as four to six depending on the song- then split them left and right, on almost everything. You're trying to make all these different guitars sound like one GREAT big, fat guitar coming out of a radio, and if there's a solo during the song, you need that solo to be able to cut above everything else. If you use your arsenal of tones on the body of the track, the solo's not going to be able to come out, so you have to save that one special solo amp, which was a Marshall Bogner. So we would work up the track using the Les Pauls and Fenders and Marshalls, and then save the Bogner for the solo. Typically, Dave's 4-12 Marshall cabinet also had a combination of a 57 and a RE-20 in front of it."

During tracking, Navarro offered Guitar Player a partial look at his favored axes to play on record, sharing his memory of using "Gibson Les Pauls for most of Nothing's Shocking, plus a Kramer. But I don't remember everything because I was in a drug haze at the time. I've pawned and rented so many guitars that I never really paid attention to that stuff." Filling in the blanks, engineer Ronnie Champagne added that in the studio "Dave had 3 or 4 different tones: the Les Paul through the

Marshall crunchy sound; then a clear Fender sound, just brighter and more open; another sound we utilized was a Tube Driver distortion guitar pedal, which I ran through a clean Fender amp, which sounded AMAZING to Dave when he first heard it because he didn't come from that school of trying to get a crunchy sound by hitting a clean amp hard. Dave also got a lot of big, open dreamy quality sounds through the Marshall/Les Paul using a delay, which Dave did a lot on that record. All these guitar sounds were used on every song throughout the album."

When Navarro turned his attention to the album's brilliant solo work, the engineer detailed that "Dave did his solos in the control room, usually sitting down on a couch, and I'd run his guitar through the wall directly into the amps on the other side. He'd play back through big monitors so he could get the feedback, etc he wanted from his guitars like he would be standing out in front of them. Most guitar players use their guitars and the amp and what comes off of the amp to get that magic thing that goes on, and when you're sitting in the control room, it's a little hard to do that, because you're not next to your amp, you're not in the line of fire. But he pulled it off." Not surprisingly, as it had been with rhythms, Champagne added that Farrell's presence was always looming, "within the overdubbing process, for solos, Perry would get really specific at times about what he wanted, which could frustrate Dave because he thought he was already giving Perry the parts he wanted leading up to the solos. On the solos, I think Dave was eager to get into a little more of what HE wanted to do, and so there was a little friction going on there between he and Perry at times. There were four of us in the room- myself, Dave Jerden, Perry and Dave Navarro, and there were things going on where we were doing stuff to make it interesting where the tension wouldn't rise to the level where everyone wanted to go home. We got through it at the end of the day."

When the studio team of Farrell, Jerden and Champagne began work on Perry Farrell's vocals, Jerden highlighted Perry's co-producer role with his recollection that during recording, "one area I stayed out of, as far as Jane's Addiction went, was Perry's vocals, he even mixed his own vocals. I stayed busy with everything else, and let him deal with his vocals." Engineer Ronnie Champagne added that Farrell required such freedom from any and all recording conventions because "vocalists like Perry make their own rules, and its all new- he's not like a lot of other sings that stand in a spot and give you a performance. We were in experimental mode for a lot of the vocals, and we sacrificed some technical norms (i.e. doing it correctly) for something else (i.e. the performances) that you heard for the first time ever on the finished product that became *Nothing's Shocking*. For instance, Perry's process of doubling himself was not doubling like let's say clean, in that sense of huge doubled vocals, but a lot of the ones we hear later weren't intentional as being doubles, but sounded good enough with each other that we wound up going with them. There's a little bit of that element going on there. We also used a lot of Perry's scratch vocals on the final mixes for that album, but we also did a lot of expansive overdubbing. Perry's not Pavarotti, but he has an equally as unique voice, that put out the right way is as powerful as Pavarotti's, just a different approach. Perry took his craft very seriously, but that said, we tried some crazy shit while tracking- one example was where he ran at the microphone screaming at it on 'Had a Dad.' A lot of experimentation, where our reasoning was 'We've gone this far, we might as well open door X."

Offering Farrell's signature multi-tracked lead and harmony vocals as an example of the singer's entirely unique and unorthodox recording style in the studio, producer Dave Jerden explained that "when he sings and does harmonies, he hears harmonies in his head. So when he sings, he'll sing one line, do one pass, and he may stay on the root note, and then go to a third, and then a fifth, and then the next take, he'll kind of invert the thing, he'll start with the third, and then go to the root note. And maybe he'll do like 4, 5 maybe 6 takes, he has all the harmonies going. So it may sound like it was just one track doing a third, and one track doing a fifth, but they're all jumping around. And because I couldn't say to him 'Ok, now let's do a harmony, and do a 3rd on this track..' Cause like, with most artists, I'll lay down a basic vocal track, then I'll do harmonies. Perry wouldn't know what I was talking about, so what I did was just let him sing it the way he wanted to sing it, and that way, mistakes and all, we'll just deal with it later. And that's what we did, and in the mix, we took out the bad parts. Normally I clean that stuff up as we go along. So what I was doing was working with Dave Navarro on guitars, and working with Steven Perkins and Eric Avery, and then Perry had this delay unit, where, when he was doing vocals, he also laid down the delay units as he sang. So I'd let him do any kind of effects he wanted, because I knew that was important to really pull it off. He's not a very technical singer, totally raw. He had complete autonomy over his vocals though." Engineer Champagne added that "as far as little parts went, There's SO MANY different layers of vocals on those records, because in some cases, we liked something but it didn't quite work, then Perry would say 'Let's try an echo on it,' and suddenly it was like 'Work's now!', and we'd add it in. That went for the broader songs as well, because there were times where we had throw-away stuff from each song, and the decision of what wound up staying vs. going was made by the track. The track tells you if it works or not, especially with a band as experimental as Jane's Addiction, because a lot of the accent parts helped round out the songs."

Atmospherically, engineer Champagne shared his memory that "Perry liked lights low, incense, lots of ambience," while adding of Farrell's technical set-up that "Perry has this little rack that he uses, and at that time it was a Yamaha SPX 90 and his Ibanez Delay, and he used the SPX 90 more like a fattener than a doubler, and I designed this one patch for him that you could tune in stereo, and you had a left and right pair that you could detune from the center. So I would detune the left side 3 percent, and uptune the right side 3 percent, so though it was out of tune, it sounded in tune. It was very unscientific, and also made his voice very alien-sounding in a David Bowie or Peter Gabriel-kind of way, and allowed Perry to use his voice as a effect, whether it was delays, chorusing, modulation, feedback, etc, which is what he'd use his Ibanez for. Going into that rig, we miced him up with a combination of the 58 going through the gear, plus an 87 he sang into directly. So the way we set it up was him standing at the 58, with the 87 just above him pointing down at him and recording simultaneously. So he was screaming and yelling and doing his thing into the 58 with all the effects going, but was also being captured in a live sense unaffected by the 87. So with the two tracks, we had the 58 running with effects going while he recorded, and the 87 dry so we could use that to effect the vocals any way we wanted."

Elaborating further on the selection of a U-87 to track the powerhouse singer, Champagne recalled that "just prior to making that record, I had recorded some jazz stuff with Paul Degray, and we came up with these techniques of micing the singer's lower back to get to get a resonance, and then having a really nice mic in front, like a U-87 and also a dynamic in front- like a SM-7 or a 56. Something someone can scream into and I don't have to worry about distortion. The problem using a U-87 on a guy like Perry is, the closer he got to the mic, it was always trying to get that fine balance between where he was going to break up the gear- where its gonna distort the equipment- because literally when you put too much pressure on a big diaphragm like that, it stops working, and makes a really nasty sound. Its not meant to handle that kind of pressure, so basically I used a combination of the dynamic mics and the 87 on Perry. I remember him doing some really crazy stuff, like he'd start at one end of the room- and I'd have the microphone hanging upside down at an angle where the diaphragm would be pointed kind of at the center of his nose- and then the dynamic would be in front- and he'd run toward the mix when screaming a part like the 'bugaboo' part in 'Had a Dad.' There's a lot of little things like that we did with him that were abnormal because what he was doing was abnormal, punk. It wasn't Frank Sinatra singing in there, it was more like: 'He's moving around a lot, and I have to figure out a way to keep the mic in front of his face.' And I didn't want to hold it, because then I was going to get handling noise."

Delving further into the creation of some of the album's classic cuts, beginning by recalling the inspiration behind the legendary album opener '*Mountain Song*'- which Billboard Magazine deemed "one of alt-rock's greatest anthems," - Perry Farrell shared with a rock journalist his memory of when "I first came to L.A., I would go up to Laurel Canyon, I'd look down at the lights at night... I'd say 'I bet every one of these motherfuckers will know my name.'...Every little fuckin' house way up there on top of that mountain. Feels good now." For bassist Eric Avery, he singles out the song as his favorite off the album because "it was the first thing Perry and I came up with (pre-Janes) and I love Dave's guitar solo at the key change." Navarro, for his own part, shared with Guitar World that the song served as his catalyst for joining the band, recounting the day "they gave me a tape, and I heard a few songs and really liked them. Stephen picked me up from my apartment in Westwood and took me over to Perry's place. That was the first time I met Perry. He opened the door and said, 'Hey!' He was really excited and happy - and really young. We went inside and started playing a groove which is now referred to as *'Mountain Song.'* Perry said, 'Wow, that sounds completely different. And from that point on, I was in.' " Drummer Steve Perkins added in an interview with Ink 19 that his favorite part of the song being its layered rhythms, explaining that at first listen, "if you look at the rhythm in *'Mountain Song'*; the bass. Eric doesn't leave much room for me, because he's playing every note. But I know there is room for me, so while he's doing that I go and I play between everything. All of sudden, he's got a rhythm and I've got a rhythm, so it sounds like there's two or three rhythms happening. I keep my hi-hat going the whole time -- so there's another rhythm. Then Perry's percussive vocals and Dave's rhythms (come along). It takes a good ear to understand Jane's Addiction sometimes because maybe it sounds like a lot to digest, because there are so many poly-rhythms, especially live. Live, we all really start working off each other, and it's not as tame or as controlled as a studio environment. The craft behind Jane's Addiction is so powerful and potent."

Every rock band has a ballad, usually one that helps their commercial breakthrough for the rare club of bands who ever gain admittance into the mainstream. With Jane's Addiction, that moment came with *'Jane Says'* off their debut LP 'Nothing's Shocking.' Written as an ode to ex-housemate Jane Bainter, Perry Farrell recalled aiming in the song's writing to capture a story every listener could relate to in some way, sharing his opinion with BAM that "I think we picked a great subject, because Jane is a very beautiful woman (in her heart). She could also be called 'Plain Jane.' -- Thick glasses, very outcast, very insecure, a lot like us here. I look at her like a tragic figure. She's a Smith graduate, she's extremely intelligent, which is very unappealing to most men. She still hasn't found love, which is pretty much like us...Every time I see Jane she's just not quite right, but she's always hopeful that something great is about to happen. 'I'm gonna kick tomorrow.' Every time I see her, I just feel like I wanna cry. She's a very warm person; she'd give you her last apple if it was in her sack of lunch. At the same time, no one really appreciates her and she can't quite get herself together. She's one of these people that lives slightly out of linear time. There's us and then there's Jane. She can talk to you and she can see you, but she's always slightly somewhere else. I don't know, maybe everybody feels like that and that's probably why people can relate to that song." Elaborating on his affections for the song, Perry added in a 1987 WB press interview as among his reasons the fact that "it's got the name of the band in it. And it's a real, real 'Hollywood' song. It's funny that you're talking about Jane because I was just with her last night. And we were doing interviews with Jane. And it's also about a close friend, so I guess that puts a spot in your heart. That'll always be there. Jane is like the sweetest girl in the world if you ever met her. There is a real softness in my heart for that song."

Of the thundering *'Ocean Size,'* Perry shared of its autobiographical inspiration that the song was "about being homeless. It was written-- I lived in a house, an eight room house, that was occupied by about, let say, 14 people. And they were all clean, every one of them. They always did the dishes and always kept the house very well groomed. All musicians. And we were kicked out of the place. They told us to move. We had to evacuate. And I was just at that time in my life, I was sick of moving. Because, you know, I'm sure you've gone through the experience of having to go looking for apartments and stuff. And it's really difficult for a guy like myself to show up and try to, you know, pass myself off as a normal, dependable young man who's not going to screw up this guy's house when I leave. And the lyrics, if you think about being homeless, or having to leave your home, is 'I wish I was ocean size. They can not move you, no one tries. No one pulls you out from your home, like a tooth aching a jawbone.' "

Recounting the message behind *'Pigs in Zen'* in an interview with journalist Dave Thompson, Perry Farrell revealed that when researching the song's concept, "I read the *Gita*, I read *Black Magic Crowley*, the *Bible*, anything I could get my hands on. If you want to talk about reaching nirvana, reaching Zen, well, the pig is closer than we are because the pig doesn't have material possessions. He fucks when he wants to, he eats when he's hungry, and he sleeps when he's tired. That's the whole point of Zen. That's exactly what pigs do... so, *'Pigs in Zen.'* " Elaborating on the song's roots, the singer recalled in an interview with Words/Music that "I had a band previous to this that was involved with Hinduism. And they abstained from sex. And they abstained from meat. In other words, they abstained from enjoying themselves. Anything that would be in the nature of self-enjoyment, they abstained from. The only time they would have sex would be under the laws marriage and that would be to give pleasure to Krishna. It would be for Krishna and you would not be able to enjoy it yourself. And I just about had enough of that. And the band broke up and I was, at the time, really, really just angry about it all. Because I had a great band on my hands. I had great musicians and we really could've done something. It was a band with integrity. But this whole Krishna thing just got in the way completely. And it really split the band up. So I wrote *'Pigs In Zen'* because they were talking about reaching this state of nirvana where you're in a state of bliss and you don't need anything. Well, a pig doesn't need clothes. A pig-- he's exactly where they want to be. It's what's humans are striving for... to be pigs. And they don't realize it. That's what humans-- I mean, it's funny that they pull all these things in to make themselves happy but it makes them unhappy. Because all those things that they pull in... all these-- the more you grab in, it's like the more you lose-- the more you have at stake to lose. You know, every possession is yet another possession that you may lose. And a pig having none and just being happy... laying in the mud. And a pig shits, eats when it's hungry, and it has sex when it's horny, and it sleeps when it's tired. And it pays no bills. So there you have it." Producer Dave Jerden counted the song as among his favorites, sharing his observation that "on the first record, there were lots of performances that were just great musicianship. Particularly, off of *Nothing's Shocking* was *'Pigs in Zen'*, because everything you hear was done in one take, and that was it. We didn't do any overdubs or anything."

For the beautiful *'Summertime Rolls,'* engineer Ronnie Champagne- offering fans an inside look into Farrell's most intimate creative moments during tracking for the song's vocals- shared that "in *'Summertime Rolls,'* on that line where he's singing 'Summer, summer, summer, summer, summer, summer, summer, summer, summer' over and over again, and little fairy voices, and psych-acoustic kind-of trips, a lot of that came when we were listening back through the 3 takes I recorded of his lead vocal, so there's 6 tracks right there, and each time Perry did a lead take, one was WILDLY different from another, and we would pick from different highlights among them and comp together our vocal master." The engineer further recalled of its recording that "we switched up the way we recorded the drums by going down to a smaller-size kit, because we used tympanis on one of those songs, and had to change the kit to get the tympani in there, so Steve could play it while he was playing the rest of the song. We didn't think of that before we set up the mics, one day this tympani just showed up at the studio and I was like 'What the fuck? Where am I going to put these?' But we made it work, and were near the end of tracking at that point, so we were able to strip the drum set down a little to make it fit. Additionally, on *'Summertime Rolls,'* the guitar tone with the echo was recorded that way, but we added a lot of overdubbing of little accent parts later." Sharing how the haunting *'Had a Dad'* evolved from demo stages to the final version laid during principle tracking, drummer Steven Perkins recalled that the band's original version of the song "is a version Warner Bros. rejected because it had piano and chimes and backward sounds on it and goes into some very weird places. It's definitely a journey, and we always liked that version better." Sharing in the same WB press interview that heading back into the studio "we had tried some new ideas, and we thought we'd really achieved something. This version has lots off cool textures, as opposed to the more rock thing that Warner's was looking for. Now, the people at Warners love the track!"

Arguably the album's most provocative and inherently controversial cut, *'Ted, Just Admit It,'* which Billboard hailed as for being sonically "stretched to epic proportions, making great use of changing moods and dynamics (something most alt-rock bands of the time were oblivious to)." Constructing a ground-breaking narrative that took on both exploitive media sensationalism surrounding of serial killers and the phenomenon the press makes them with wall-to-wall coverage, where as Farrell so correctly observed at the time: "and the news is just another show." Recalling his specific inspiration for the song's lyrical subject matter, the singer recounted to Melody Maker that "I guess I wrote all that during a 'sex is violent' mode of thinking. At the time I was looking at movies about serial killers and there was a repetition to the way they all acted out their murders, an underlying thing of sex. For people like them, its all really apparent. For people that are so called sane, its less obvious. But I doubt its any less there. I think they're just more in control of it." More specifically, Perry added to BAM that " *'Ted...'* was written without the thought of music. It was written right at the moment I was frying on acid and watching a video called MURDER: NO APPARENT MOTIVE. And it was just interviews with murderers. And, of course, you got to relive the dastardly deed through dramatization. And after that I just sat down and put a melody behind it. But it was good because I had a chance to see what the words did and then put music to accompany the words, rather than vice versa, which is the way a lot of let's just say bad rock bands will work. They'll start with the song, then hurry up and throw words down on top of it."

In authenticating the song to the extreme of including a live sample of serial killer Ted Bundy's voice, Perry explained to a rock journalist that the move was a risky one from the jump, such that "I lifted the stuff from a video, and I don't want to name it as we might get in trouble. We were supposed to get approval on it, but we never did-I guess we just ran out of time." Engineer Ronnie Champagne recalled of the technical process of sampling Bundy's voice, "I got a video recorder from my house, got a video interview with Ted Bundy, cued it up to the spot where Bundy was saying all those things Perry wanted, and recorded it onto a 2 track. After that, I just stood at the 2-track with my thumb on the reel, waited until Perry nodded, then let my thumb go and that's how we flew it in. Took a couple times till we got it right, and boom that was it. I knew that song was going to be so special from that moment."

Farrell added of his decision to address the song directly to Bundy in the form of its invitational title, *'Ted, Just Admit it,'* that he'd done so because "he never admitted to his guilt. Within the song, there were a lot of ideas. Its about what the media does to the mind. The concept to that song, in my mind, sums up the spirit of the times." Those times were also addressed within the song's lyrics in arguably Farrell's sharpest editorial on the aforementioned sensationalist media reporting to date, with Perry pointing out that "bizarre shit like that goes on every single day. There's a TV program called 'Current Affair' they show, and it has the most psychotic things, like some 12 year old kid who strangled his friends mother with a dog chain because he saw 'Friday the 13th' and thought he could get away with it because Jason gets away with everything. Just the weirdest, sickest shit you see in America every day." Musically, bassist Eric Avery shared in an interview with Guitar Player that to match the song's climatic ending, he used "a Fender Heavy pick, but not always. The end of *'Ted, Just Admit It'* gets really violent and unstructured, and I slap--not like funk guys do, just for the brighter, more violent sound. No precision, just angry. I've always tried to avoid the luxury of relying on effects to make things interesting. It makes me work harder, I think."

When principle production wrapped and the team transitioned to mixing, for engineer Ronnie Champagne, the process was a relatively seamless one, recalling that "basically my job during recording was to give Dave Jerden enough stuff to have as much fun with as he could, and with the amount of tracks we had to play with, which was 48 at that time. Dave presented it to me like this when we started recording, 'Give me it all, give me all the fucking shit, all the crap, everything. That's what filters are for, you carve that stuff out. If you don't have it, you can't do anything.' So as the engineer recording the album, it was up to me to get Dave everything as producer he needed." From co-producer Perry Farrell's sonic perspective, with *'Nothing's Shocking,'* he explained at the time that he and the band were trying "create something close to the heartbeat, maybe some kind of fucked-up heartbeat. We aim for the center of the chest."

The label was on entirely the same page with the band, as engineer Ronnie Champagne explaining that "Warner Bros. at that moment was a nurturing element for artists, and we were getting feedback from the label as we were handing in mixes, 'Can you make it bigger?' And it wasn't like what we were giving them was weak, it was already over the top, its just once they heard how over the top it was, they wanted more. The competition back then was Guns N' Roses, you had to beat that, and Warner wanted to change gears in the rock world, and Warners was VERY aware of the potential Jane's had and were imagining that kind of impact was possible. They were looking at it like: this is another Jimi Hendrix; this is another Led Zeppelin."

Conceding that at the time no one was quite sure exactly what they had on their hands, everyone universally believed it was revolutionary enough a sound to warrant blind faith in, with the engineer adding that "at that point, I don't think any of us realized just how fucking BIG that record was going to be in terms of sonics. I mean, Dave had to learn how to mix that record as he went, because it wasn't typical... this was a first time, out of the box gig as far as the MASSIVE amount of tracks and massive amount of sound to deal with, and it just kept getting bigger and bigger and bigger. So it was like: shit man, can we make it any bigger? Well, let's try at least. The beauty of the way we recorded it was when the band broke down the lightest, fluffiest angelic stuff, it was all there and was pristine like a jazz record. That was the cool part, because it went from being a really clean-sounding jazz record to completely over-the-top, in your face Marshall guitars and bashing, that was the beauty of it- that's what we tried to accomplish. Because there's a lot of records out there that don't go up and down, and we were trying to go for: let's get their attention, and then scare the fuck out of them!"

Perry seemed equally as eager to re-shape the rock masses with his masterpiece, sharing with journalists Al and Lawrence Livermore at the time that "I myself am ready for something else. Not different than what I'm doing, but I'm ready for a change in the attitude of the youth. I would like to attempt to start a new attitude slightly. More of getting together, and easing up on each other. It's all got to be torn down again and started over," adding to another journalist that "What we're going to do is blow people away. When we get out there, we're going to do things no one else has ever done. Musically, we're already light-years ahead."

Recalling that- not surprisingly- "Perry was a big influence on the mixing," creating along with his co-producer what Rolling Stone Magazine concluded were "flights into dreamy psychedelia," engineer Ronnie Champagne shared of Dave Jerden's mixing style that "Dave paints in LOUD colors as a mixer," with Jerden himself adding that "I believe producing records is no different from painting a picture, conceptually its the same strategies that are used in painting a picture. It has to do with balance, all the rules of art, of shading, light, perspective, everything, plus colors. Its the same thing, you have to know how to put the sounds together. I don't hear what I'm doing, I actually see it. There's a mental picture I get." For Perry Farrell, ultimately with his sonic vision he sought to create a collage where "we're forcing heavy-metal dudes and Mohawk dudes and young girls and blacks to all get I the same room and actually open up and its really great. I love looking out and seeing the Mohawk guy in the pit with the skinhead and some guy wearing a Joy Division T-shirt hanging out with some older guy who's maybe in college- a really healthy, eclectic crowd." Indeed, the New York Times would later comment that "At live shows, Jane's Addiction unites disparate subcultures as successfully as it melds musical influences. Its audience is a bizarre coalition of metal fans, punks, college-radio hipsters, goths, nouveau hippies and the unaligned and curious. What attracts such a motley array of fans is that the band has managed to bring back a sense of rock-and-roll as an underground."

Unleashed on August 23rd, 1988, the rock world fell instantly under the spell of *'Nothing's Shocking,'* with Rolling Stone Magazine granting Perry his first wish to of achieving a perfect "blend (of)...funk and metal- that's...what Zeppelin was doing," by concluding in their review of the LP that "Jane's Addiction is the true heir to Led Zeppelin, creating music that's simultaneously forbidding and weighty, delicate and ethereal. But...Jane's Addiction's version of Zeppelin is stripped of Robert Plant's fairy-tale whimsy: even when the sound is contemplative and plaintive, the sensibility is hardheaded and realistic." Taking the derivative comparisons one step beyond Zeppelin, Buzz Magazine also compared the band to "Led Zeppelin, U2, and the Culture Club," further noting that "this band is meant to hit everybody where it hurts." For guitarist Dave Navarro, the latter honor was one he would admit to Guitar Player took him years after the fact to get used to, explaining that "I see why people compare us to Zeppelin, although it's frustrating at times. We've got a strong front guy, a brilliant drummer, and a lot of different sides. We can be pretty or loud. Still, we never dreamed that anyone would ever compare us to Led Zeppelin."

As authentically as he spoke for and to the youth, evinced by the L.A. Times observation that "what these songs show is a gritty street reality as seen through the haze of troubled adolescence," the reviewer seemed surprised to "find that Farrell is not an adolescent at all." Ahead of their time, Perry Farrell and Jane's Addiction marched to a rhythm on their debut LP that Music Connection noted moved at "a...psychotic tempo," adding that "Jane's Addiction takes its audience into a whirling, drug-induced state of (un)consciousness." Indeed, as drummer Steven Perkins- in an interview with journalists Al and Lawrence Livermore- summarized the band as they raced toward the dawn of alt-rock's mainstream, "it comes down to three things: the friendship, the music, and (our fans)... that's what the movement is all about. Jane is like a Porsche; fast and mean." Drum Magazine would arguably sum the band's position up best heading into the close of the 1980s, noting that because of "their unpredictable, high-energy, and sometimes gender-bending look, along with their sonic mix of punk, funk, and metal, presented the audience with a unique sound and presaged the rise of alternative music that would later arise in the form of grunge-rock acts like Nirvana and Pearl Jam."

"Jane's Addiction's *Ritual De Lo Habitual* (1990) was too revealing for some retailers, due to male and female nudity (not shown). In protest of the album being pulled, singer Perry Farrell issued this white cover quoting the First Amendment." - MTV.com

" I'm looking for more of a forceful optimism in the decade to come." - Perry Farrell, 1990

"Producer Dave Jerden, with his uncanny ability to make the group sound bigger than God." - Billboard Magazine

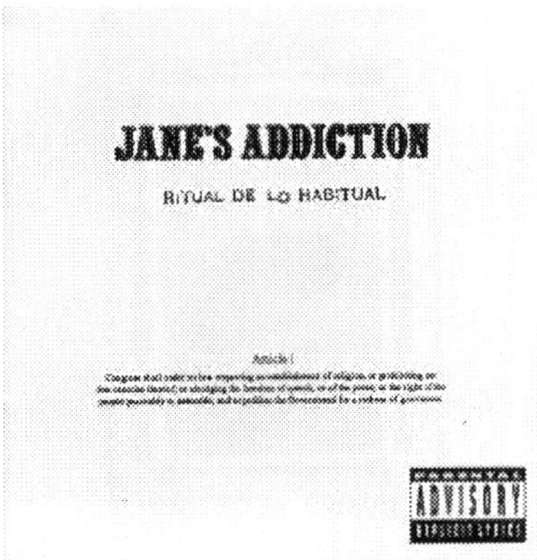

Part IV: Ritual De Lo Habitual

With the release of the band's sophomore album- and commercial breakthrough- *Ritual De Lo Habitual* in 1991, Jane's Addiction would crystallize their stature as the Supreme Being in Alternative rock like a Greek statue, immortalized in time and worshiped by millions, not just in that generation, but for many to follow. And did they follow. As alternative rock's sacrificial Jesus, Farrell was authentically viewed by his followers as a holy figure, that is a prophet who had a vision that made sweeping sense to a large population who in turn embraced it as their own. His mantic prose gave listeners a fervent sense of identity and relevance to define their own times, rather than allowing the establishment to, as Farrell set forth in *Classic Girl*, explaining that "they may say- those were the days, but in a way, for us, you know, for us *THESE* are the days." Jane's Addiction's fans followed the band like lost tribe seeking deliverance, and evolved exponentially in numbers as a movement over the course of the band's first and second albums. Via *Ritual De La Habitual*, Farrell took what had become the band's own underground in the late 1980s into the mainstream in 1991 with a traveling summer festival that Farrell described as "kind of a rock & roll circus."

Where the hippie movement had Woodstock, alternative rock had Lollapalooza, a Festival Perry Farrell clearly envisioned as larger than himself or his band because they used the debut year of the festival as their farewell tour. It was his generation's exodus to a legitimacy of community Rock had not known in decades, passionately embodying its culture, music, politics, and times. Farrell knew the band had done its job in utilizing their commercial cross-over to jump-start a new pop culture, rather than become part of a pre-existing one. The band wasn't seeking to expand, rather redefine completely, opening rock fans' minds to a new consciousness that bled all musical sub-genres, cultures and fan bases into one unified awareness through Lollapalooza. Voted by Spin magazine as the #1 tour that changed the world, Farrell explained at the time that "I'm staying with rock music. To me that includes rap, industrial, what some would call noise bands, what some would call the Seattle sound. The rock-funk thing. I'm just looking to do an overview of rock & roll...(But also, as a multimedia event), using music, art, and military discoveries and weaponry as forms of entertainment...There was alot of thought about mixing and making (the bands) into a multifaceted bill...I wanted to integrate- racially integrate, musically integrate- and I think its a good start."

Where the considerable popularity of hard rock and heavy metal throughout the 1980s had kept the fundamental foundation of rock n' roll alive for Jane's to launch from commercially in the context of accessibility to the generic rock fan, the band was still aiming for the brain- rather than the crotch- which implied a massive conversion in focus would be required to win over the metal heads. It came with the end of the 1980s, and a coat of hair metal saturation so heavy that even the weakest rock mind was giving off a distress signal, looking for some alternate musical stimuli. For the millions of America's youth who had represented the true underbelly of anything mainstream in the 1980s, be it their popularity-status socially in high school or with girls, or be it an abused home they had to return to after being scorned at school, they truly had nowhere to turn to- not even in the last frontier of escape, music. Those kids needed a savior, not a buddy to party with. They didn't want to escape their problems so much as they sought a musical confidant to understand them, and ultimately to lead them through musical therapy to escape. Jane's Addiction was that adviser, and Perry Farrell's lyrical gift held a mystical wisdom and profound relevance for his listeners that Nelson's *After the Rain* or Faster Pussycat's *House of Pain* was never capable of. Alternative rock became America's mainstream in 1991 not because of a trend kids were generically following, but because of a specific message they understood intimately as it was their own.

Jane's Addiction was a public mirror in this way for the personal yearnings of America's youth, as well as the voice who finally understood the substance of their cry for help. Nirvana was the second generation of that reflection, and virtually every legend thereafter from the Grunge era of rock readily credits Perry Farrell as their Godfather. Stone Temple Pilots/ Velvet Revolver's lead singer Scott Wetland qualified the latter in an interview, explaining that "I grew up on people who were all about visually overloading the senses, whether it's Bowie or Freddie Mercury or the New York Dolls - all the way up to Jane's Addiction. Jane's were my heroes when I was in my late teens and early 20s. I was still living in Huntington Beach and I'd drive up to see them at Scream and other clubs. What they were doing was just magical to me. I saw elements of everything I loved about art-rock - that flamboyance, the sheer insanity of it all...I think Stone Temple Pilots, Nirvana, and Pearl Jam actually owe something (major) to Jane's Addiction...(Jane's) pretty much saved Rock n Roll for me...*Nothing's Shocking*...was one of those records that made me believe, that became my bible and taught me everything." Soundgarden singer and lead songwriter Chris Cornell echoed Weiland's sentiment, explaining in an interview with Spin Magazine that "I think a lot of people out there in Seattle think that rock'n'roll changed in the early '90s when

Nirvana showed up, and everyone had a big hit. But it didn't really work that way...Jane's Addiction laid the groundwork. Musically, Jane's had a huge impact on Soundgarden." For Farrell personally, the precipice alternative rock sat at thanks in large part to the sound he had co-founded with Jane's was a movement he explained at the time to a rock journalist he was "proud of," adding that "I hope the alternative people are always surprised when they hear my music. These people have their ear to the street, and they're always waiting for something else. Metal people are willing to hear something else, but there's a format there. The fact that metal people like (Ritual) is more a reflection on the state of metal than it is from us angling the product. it's a good sign, though, and about fucking time."

Hailed at the time by the San Francisco Chronicle as "a ferocious-beautiful force of nature," channeling that energy onto tape was a sonic journey that for Farrell, was a musical vision he'd had "(in my head) for a long time. I've been waiting to achieve (it) for five years, and now, here it is. It's the end of a five-year project, and everything's peaking." Because the album had been in the works for the better part of 5 years, drummer Steve Perkins shared with Modern Drummer, "the Jane's tunes were written at the same time...(So) *'Three Days'* might have been written on the same day as 'Had A Dad,' a song on a different album. But we definitely want all the songs to sound different." As with the band's debut, bassist Eric Avery shared in an interview with Guitar Player his recollection that "*Ritual* was written mostly by Perry--it just came down that way, because we've been spending a lot less time in the same room together. He'd come in with a basic chord progression, humming the riffs. Then we'd get a bass line, then David would work the guitar over it." For Navarro, his goal with the record, as recounted in an interview with journalist Gary Graff, was "to show the progression of the band from the last album. As a foursome we had become a little bit more cohesive in terms of playing together. We had certainly expanded some of our parameters, and I think that we just tried to accomplish capturing that by still maintaining our raw, live feel."

Recording got off- quite literally- to a rocky start when engineer Ronnie Champagne recalled that "in between *Nothing's Shocking* and

Ritual, we had a huge earthquake, which pretty much toasted the old Hollywood Post Office building El Dorado Studio had been housed in, ruined the foundation of the building to the point where they deemed it uninhabitable. So we leased a room at Track Record up in the Valley, and when we first moved in there, the studio had a Trident console in a nice big wood room for recording drums, and then on the other side, he had a warehouse he was converting into a studio. It was a really big, live room with 30 foot ceilings, a really crazy shaped room with a glassed-in control room built into it, and we took that over soon after, took all the gear from the old El Dorado studio and put the Neve 8232 console and everything else into that newly-finished room, and that became the main Jane's studio for Ritual."

Because the songs were already so rehearsed from being performed on the road, engineer Ronnie Champagne recalled that heading into recording, "we did like a mini-preproduction for Ritual, where the guys had pretty much already dialed in the songs, and knew what they were going to do as far as what the parts were. The songs for Ritual were already written and had been performed all through the Nothing Shocking tour. Not only were the parts fleshed out, but not only that, circumstances what they were, Perry maybe backed off a little from *Nothing's shocking.* It was a different dynamic on that record." As what the engineer thought was the start of recording commenced, Champagne shared that "we set everything up and had started tracking drums and bass tracks for about 10 days, then Perry came in, said 'This is not what I want, this is not what I'm talking about,' and we stopped working on the record for a couple months."

Once the band got back on track and re-entered Track Record to begin proper work on the album, Champagne recalled that "we were on lock-out for months and months and months. We didn't really have any budgetary constraints recording the album, and I would say that record had no less than a $500,000 budget." Detailing the production team's technical set-up for recording, the engineer added that "Dave Jerden and I were all excited because we'd gotten a new digital Sony Dash 48 track tape machine, and were trying to get the level of product bumped up by getting rid of the tape machine hiss. Because we were working on

Nothing's Shocking, the amount of noise was shocking. So on the second record, what we did was still used the 2-inch 800 Studer 16 track analog tape machine to do the drums and bass, then at the same time, we were dumping down on to a Mitsubishi 32 Track, and then did a lot of the guitar and vocal overdubs on the Sony 48 Track. In the control room, the console was great for recording rock, the mics were awesome, and the control room was really nice, big and loud as shit. We were using a 3-way monitor system, where you have two 15's and a wide dispersion horn, which was typically back then."

Intensely focused on the task at hand throughout recording, though Dave Jerden shared with Details Magazine that, in a departure from the first album, "mostly the guys would come in and lay their parts down themselves," when the band's individual members showed up to record, "in the studio, it was really about getting the record done. With Jane's, there was never any parties going on, it was so intense on a different level that it didn't attract the partying entourage you'd usually see back then. I was there 5 hours before anyone ever showed up, doing editing, back-ups, all the shit you'd normally do in prep of a session. And Id have all that out of the way by 11 o'clock in the morning, then Steve Perkins would show up and we'd get something to eat, then screw around in the afternoon and make sure everything was working."

Jane's Addiction secret weapon, musically-speaking, has always been drummer Steven Perkins, Drum Magazine hailed as "one of rock's most unique drummers. Known best for his work with famed alternative band Jane's Addiction, Perkins' use of poly-rhythms and incorporation of tribal elements separates him from many of his contemporaries." Perkins spoke first-hand on his sense rhythm to Guitar Center, explaining that as a player "there's something infectious about music and its rhythm. It's like a heartbeat or a pulse. When you go to sleep, when you wake up, when you eat–there's rhythm everywhere; it's part of our lives. And if you can capture it and make people feel it, that's the power."

In the course of harnessing that power in the studio, engineer Ronnie Champagne recalled that "Steve's drum set-up- Steve's drums changed for *Ritual*. On *'Nothing's Shocking'*, we had the whole kettle drum and just a massive kit, but for Ritual, he had a really tight core of a kit, and he started using a DW with rims on it, which made the tones of the toms exemplary, because before he'd been using this old Ludwig kit with the bottoms and heads off. The whole thing about drums if you have push and the pull going through the actual wood itself, it dampens the drums so much so that its actually harder to tune because its being warped by the amount of weight that's being held on that little part of the wood. Well, if you take that same drum and put a set of hanging rims on it, the drum turns into a whole different instrument and becomes a big singing thing, its really cool. Because we now had the toms on hangers, we didn't have bottom mic a lot of things because they sounded great by themselves. We would use 421s on the tops, which I thought sounded a little rounder and little more tomish than the 57s, and we'd switched from the 57s because with the Mitsubishi tape machine, they were just too much."

Steven Perkins shared with rock journalist Mike Dolbear that while "I definitely do my own tuning...when I get into the studio, I listen to the engineer. I don't want to tell him what mics to use, I don't want to tell him where to place them, I don't want to tell him how much tape or pillows to use. I want to see what he's got. He spends his whole life in that room, what tricks does he have! I know what it sounds like out here because my ears are next to my drums, but it'll sound different in the control room. It might sound great to me, but an engineer might have to say, 'Dude, the mic is different to your ears and the room". I might hear a big fat sound but it comes out on record as a little 'pap'. He'll tell me it's the wrong mic, or the mic is too close and it's the wrong EQ levels. It'll become a team effort for him to get what I'm tuning for. There's always my tuning and drum set, then the co-operation between the team making it happen. I like wood rooms, some drummers like plaster and carpet, I don't cymbals sound bad in those rooms."

Elaborating on his theory on the sonic science behind the band's impeccable drum sound captured in the course of Ritual, the drummer explained to Drum World that "if I play you a tape of us in concert before we went to the studio, it's almost the same. We just played these songs as they were, under some good microphones." Engineer Ronnie

Champagne added more specifically that "for room mics, I used U-87s and an M-49 on the floor in front of the kit and half way between the wall and the kick-drum, and I also had a pair of C-12s and a C-24, which also went exactly where the M-49 was in front of the drums, with the capsule twisted. I probably got 80% of the M-49, and the rest through the C-24. On Nothing's Shocking, Dave was experimenting with the AKG, and by Ritual, I had convinced him to try the M-88 on the kick drum, and put the M-49 out front. Dependant on the song, for the Ballads, we wanted a more open kick, so we allowed the kick to go out into the room and be captured by the other mics. For the faster songs, that room noise gets in the way of the track and starts beating against the tempo, so you make a tunnel with packing blankets just to get the kick out of the room as much as possible in the front. So depending on the tempo of the song, a slower track can handle that extra reverb time with the whole warmth of the kit expanding out and breathing. We did most of the overdubbed percussion in the live room with C-12s, which were already set-up in pairs, so all you had to do was stand in a certain place and go."

According to Gibson.com, Dave Navarro, "with his six-string skills best described as a merger between heavy metal, psychedelia and modern rock...became one of alternative rock's first true guitar heroes...Navarro has proven himself one of the most versatile guitarists on the alt-rock scene of the past 25 years." Throughout recording the album that cemented that reputation, the guitarist recalled in Guitar Player that "my two...main guitars were custom built by Ibanez, and I used them for most of Ritual. Most of their guitars are real metal-looking, so I had them round off the pointy edges. They're painted with the *Nothing's Shocking* album cover. One has a start body and a Les Paul pickup configuration, because I like having the rhythm/treble toggle switch at the top. I also like having two volume knobs so I can set different levels--I'd rather do it from the guitar than a footswitch. The second guitar has a body with the top half modeled after a Telecaster but the bottom like a Les Paul cutaway. It has a hum/sing/hum pickup configuration and a 5-way switch. The pickups are ultrasonics."

In addition to his beloved Ibanezes, engineer Ronnie Champagne shared his memory that "Dave Navarro loved gear, he loved playing around with gear, and we went out to some music stores to pick out gear before we started recording *Ritual*, but Dave's main guitars on the record were lots of Ibanezes, and Dave Jerden and I had started amassing gear, so we had Telecasters, Les Pauls, and my pink Kramer Beretta 1- which we used a lot- because it had 2 settings: when the knob was pushed up, it had a single-coil Strat kind of sound, and when the knob was pushed down, it had a full-on hum bucking sound. The pick-up starter was one pick-up at that time, made in West Germany at a place called Ultrasonic, and they were reference pick-ups, which means they were really flat across your frequency range, whereas a lot of pick-ups will have different spikes in different parts of the frequency range. That can give you different tonal characteristics, where this way being flat, with the kind of metal sounds we were getting, I could really carve using the EQs on the amps, rather than on the guitars. Acoustics-wise, Dave had both a 6-string and 12-string."

Elaborating on Navarro's rig, the engineer added that "as far as amps, we used the Bogner Modified 50-Watt Marshall, now called the Snarkler, which he played along with my pink Kramer Beretta 1 on A LOT of the album's songs, and between the push-pull single coil and the hum bucking pick-up sound, we would double the sound left and right, use the humbucking as the thicker, main part of the guitar, and then get the 'chicka-chicka' single-coil sound where Dave was scratching across the strings and rock those out much chimier. I'd hook Dave's Ibanez up through a Tubedriver Stomp Box made by Chandler, and that would then go into more-or-less clean Bassman, which was awesome because it was loud and clean from the drop of a hat, as soon as you plugged in. So when we started out rhythms, if there any clean parts, they would be done through the 100-Watt Bassman with nothing else. Then for the crunchier stuff, we'd use the Tubedriver into the 100 Watt. The heavier sound of the Kramer through the Bogner would be afterward, because it was so thick that if you start out with it, the more you add to it, it just gets too much. You have to use it in such a way that you can hear different layers as a result."

Giving Navarro room to breathe on his solo parts for *Ritual,* Champagne recalled that "unlike the first record, Perry wasn't around for a lot of Dave's overdubbing, which didn't mean he wouldn't come in at later times, listen, and give his notes to me, and Dave would incorporate them later. But because those tracks had been worked on for a long time out on the road, they were already established in his mind, so when he sat down with them, it wasn't this big rush and flurry, it was more like 'Okay, here's this melody I'm going to play overtop of this rhythm,' and he'd already decided for himself or with Perry what those would be. As a result, they were much more mature than the first album, much less all over the place, much more determined. He'd really grown as a player." When laying the famously-effects layered multi-tracks of guitars that wove so beautifully throughout the fabric of the band's music, Navarro explained to Boss.com that, in the studio, "I prefer to track with my effects. I don't like to use a lot of outboard stuff. I don't like to delay my tracks after the fact. I don't like to re-amp things unless it's absolutely necessary. Basically whatever's coming out of my amp is what's going into the recorder. I pretty much want it to be the way I play it right there in the room, and I feel that if I turn it over to an engineer, it's not gonna be that way."

When attention turned to tracking the album's pulsating bass lines, the bassist began by explaining in an interview with guitar player that "the nature of the songs demanded that (a different production approach to Nothing's Shocking), the record is a lot loonier, more complicated. There are more changes, more trinkets and knickknacks. It's much more a studio album than our previous records, rather than an attempt to capture what we do live." Recalling the details of Avery's gear during recording, engineer Ronnie Champagne explained that "as far as physical basses, he played two: one was a green Fender P-bass of mine, a custom shop with noiseless pick-ups in it, and the black Fender P-bass he played on stage, the one with the stickers all over it. My bass had more of everything- more bottom, more mid, more top-end- so we used that one a lot. Eric's bass head was an SVT with the little graphic EQ on the front, he liked that because he liked to dial in the punch- that bright part of his bass like on the start of '*Three Days*.' He liked that sound when the strings were really electric. We recorded Eric with a D.I. into the console, along with 421s and RE 20s in front of the Ampeg SVT cabinet."

Correctly singled out at the time by Entertainment Weekly as "the band's guiding spirit," lead vocalist/visionary for Jane's Addiction's sound, Perry Farrell- who the Los Angeles Times commented in their review of the album "continues to convey quite masterfully traces of psychological obsession and abandon"- explained at the time that in the course of writing the album's lyrics, "I (wasn't) trying to write a novel or pre-calculated, long-term story or anything." In fact, for as plugged into his own fan culture as he was, Farrell shared with rock journalist Dave Thompson that "I don't write about current affairs or current events. I talk about things that have been going on since the beginning of time." Rather, according to the singer, his muse more centered on "a vibe, just the stuff I'm into at the moment, a mixture of it all." The result, as Spin Magazine would conclude in their review of the LP, "invites us to swim in the evocative juice of Perry's poems and in its organic, untraditional metallic presence."

Farrell's recording routine in the course of tracking what the L.A. Weekly eloquently referred to as "cosmic longhand," as engineer Ronnie Champagne recalled, consisted of "times when Perry would record later in the afternoon, and or through the evening. There was two shifts: there was the early to dinner and then late afternoon to early morning, like 4 AM. The vocal booth was his own little room with his own little set-up, he had privacy, and a little light switch where he could dim down the lights, and he had candles going, etc. We did all the vocals in one little vocal booth that had a window too off the left of the control room, and all those mics were being recorded at once so we could get multiple vocal takes at once since the mics were running to different tracks. Perry also was always twisting knobs of his effects rig as he recorded, to get the modulation effects, and he used a little bit of plate reverb on certain songs."

While some producers would have shied away from daring into the pre-digital recording territory of tracking vocals with effects running, producer Dave Jerden shared that "one thing that I do when I work is I lay my effects and everything down as I record, most guys don't. They just lay down flat sounds, I never do that. And that's from- when I first started, I only had 28 input consoles to work with, and so I had to get everything on tape. And plus, I can't hear the song grow, I want to hear the song grow. How can you tell where to layer things in, and what your next color should be and all that- its like, when you do it without putting any effects on tape, where effects are supposed to be, how can you tell where the song's going? Its like a paint by numbers, all you're doing then is drawing off drawings, since you know that a rotary sound should go here, and a flanger here, its like paint by numbers. To me it looks better if you paint as you go, because again its the serendipity of the thing. When you lay effects down as you go along, things can come out of those effects that lead you to another path. The way I work with effects is exactly the same now with digital recording as it was when we only had analog to work with. I don't use a bunch of plug ins on pro-tools, I do all my stuff as I record without board equipment. Stomp boxes, pedals on guitars, all that stuff. I hardly use any plug-ins. To me, the plug-ins sound flat, I like the sounds of outboard equipment. And putting it through outboard equipment."

As Farrell laid the intricate layers of lead and harmony vocals throughout what Billboard would later hail as "one of rock's all-time sprawling masterpieces", the engineer described a method wherein "a lot of times, Perry had already recorded the live version of what his lead vocal was going to be with the band, then within overdubbing, he had in his mind already, and so he'd listen to the track and add things, sometimes pre-plotted and other times totally off his head in the moment." Detailing Farrell's micing set-up during tracking, engineer Ronnie Champagne- using '3 Days' as an example- explained that "the opening of that song is him into an SBX 90 and the Ibanez delay, then going through the M-49 and 58 mics, along with the SM7 talk-back mic. He had a straight channel going through the SBX 90 and delay, and then we had a TC2290 effects rig that does delays and modulation so you get chorus and flanging and those types of effects. I also believe there was an AMS 16 that had a sampler on it we used as well in that song."

Presented in what Rolling Stone Magazine defined as "a hard-rockin' side and a prog-rock side," engineer Ronnie Champagne recalled that during recording "we treated the fast songs like '*Stop*' and '*Ain't No Right*' in a batch, so we got those, then did the trippier stuff in a batch."

Opening the album with an energy that quite literally kicked open the doors with the news that Jane's Addiction had arrived, *'Stop'* - the opening single and track from Ritual De Lo Habitual- would roar out of the gate and straight to # 1 on the Billboard Modern Rock chart, inspiring Billboard to hail it as among "the band's best hard rock numbers," and to take special note of guitarist Dave Navarro's "repetitive, trashy funk riff", while Rolling Stone Magazine fell instantly in love with the song's "amazing bridge." In recalling the process of writing the single, bassist Eric Avery in a conversation with Guitar Player offered it as an instance of creative serendipity where "a song may be going in a certain direction, but a mistake can happen, and we'll say, 'Wait--that works better.' An example is the slow break in *'Stop'* : Initially it was an E groove, but once I played a G instead, and it eventually became a change from E to G." Perry Farrell added of the song's lyrical message and meaning that "this is about the destruction of the world. You see, we're peace loving people. We believe we can save the world-- this band. Do you believe that?... Course not, man. You don't believe that. We can't do shit. This one's called *'Stop.'* "

Of another of the album's more energetically-paced provoca-tunes, Rolling Stone Magazine concluded that *"Ain't No Right'* admirably sums up Farrell's creed," while Perry himself added of inspiration behind the song in an interview with Face Magazine that "I have to continue to dare myself. If I don't challenge myself then I don't feel like I'm moving forward. It's like the song I wrote, *'Ain't No Right'*, where I talk about cutting myself. I did that because I thought about doing it and I was scared. So I cut myself 365 times with a razor. Aesthetically, I thought it would look cool, but, what was more important to me was the thought, 'If I can take this, then what can stop me?' " Equally as bold in his challenge on anti-discrimination anthem *'Ain't Nobody Leaving'*, Farrell reasoned with one of his live audiences in introducing the song and its message of blind equality that "you can go ahead and hate whoever the fuck you want, but the way I see it, nobody's leaving, man, so you might as well get used to it....Now, you know what I'm talking about when I say: black people are not suppressed anymore. I'm happy as hell, man. There ain't no slavery. And whether you don't like black people or Arabs, no body's leaving this city, man. Unless some mother fucking truck or a tank comes in, man, we're all here to stay. So you could be a fool and hate people or you could get used to it." To match the frantic pace of the song's rhythm, guitarist Dave Navarro recalled in a conversation with Guitar World that " in '*No One's Leaving*,' which is a pretty fast song, I threw in some very fast riffs."

Though *Ritual De Lo Habitual* had already gone gold, the release of Been Caught Stealing on October 27th, 1990 sent Jane's rocketing to the peak of the singles stratosphere, becoming their first bonafied hit single, spending 4 weeks at the # 1 spot atop the Billboard Modern Rock Singles Chart. With an accompanying smash hit video that dominated the # 1 slot on MTV's DialMTV (the Total Request Live of the 1980s) for weeks, eventually winding up # 47 on VH1's 100 Greatest Videos list. A critical darling as well from the first listen, Rolling Stone Magazine hailed the song as "a real jewel," while going on to praise the most original dance hit of the year as "a shuffling, upbeat bouncer with silly jazz chords...the song expresses a bare logic of desire that makes shoplifting seem...fun." Still, for as big a hit as the song eventually became, to producer Dave Jerden, during its creation in the studio, the producer admitted at the time "it never occurred to me that would be a single. There are songs that I like, that I think are catchy- like, when I was producing Jane's for instance, I didn't think in terms of singles at all. When I say 'thinking in terms of singles', I know that probably half the record should have stuff that's accessible. So you think in terms of length of song, and how catchy it is, so parts that are catchy- you want to make sure they reoccur in the song, and things like that."

Engineer Ronnie Champagne added of its recording that, consistent with its spontaneous rhythmic vibe, "*Been Caught Stealing'* was one that went down in one take, pretty much from beginning to end. That song had some really cool stuff on it. In the beginning, there's a really interesting guitar on it, which my guitar tech had made for me with a neck through with 12-ply laminate, made in this really nice stripes and really beautiful wood. The thing sounded amazing, you didn't even have to plug it in. It had this chime in it, and Dave used to love playing that one because it had this really wingy sound. We put that on the intro to *Been Caught Stealing*." Elaborating on Navarro's recording technique in the course of recording guitars, the engineer added his recollection that "on songs like *'Been Caught Stealing'* and *'Stop'*, a lot of times, Dave would start out playing what he was playing live, which meant he played the rhythm part up until he played the solo, did the solo, then went back to playing rhythm. So we'd listen to the solo, and go 'That sound's okay, maybe we can use that for a bit,' then we'd overdub the rhythm parts, and then go in and overdub along with his original solo. We'd go back in overdubbing and work on something if he felt it was awful he didn't want to have it there, then we'd get rid of it immediately, but a lot of the solos on that record, in principle, were recorded when he was doing his basic tracks."

Navarro added to Guitar Player of his favorite guitar part within the song's multiple stacks of tracks that "*Been Caught Stealing*' has a jangly sound that comes in a few bars after the dirty guitar part. It's three tracks of electric guitar unplugged--just a mike on the strings. It's a completely cool sound. I see music. For me, every color in the rainbow comes out of our songs. I think we're really colorful." Of the live dogs heard barking on the track, a feature of the song that Rolling Stone Magazine celebrated as "the best use of dog barks since Pet Sounds," guitarist Dave Navarro recalled in an interview with Guitar World that "we just thought it would be interesting to hear the dog on the song...So we put a microphone in the vocal booth, and when Perry went in there and started running around with the dog, he- - the dog - started barking, and that was that. It was just one of those happy accidents. It wasn't like somebody said, 'Hey let's get a dog-barking sample in here.' "

Rightly singled out as "the album's cornerstones" by Billboard in their stellar review of the album, the magazine would go onto explain of *'Three Days'* and *'Then She Did...'* that "they appear to be about an autobiographical romantic tryst between three lovers, as each composition twists and turns musically through every imaginable mood." Former girlfriend Casey Niccoli added years later to Details Magazine that indeed that third lover was Xiola, who Niccoli recalled "was Perry's lover before he met me. She was very young, very intelligent, and very beautiful. I became friends with her. She died of an overdose at nineteen. So we kind of put her on a pedestal (with *3 Days*)." Considered by most fans and critics alike to be alternative rock's equivalent of 'Stairway to Heaven,' the process of constructing the 10 minute, 49 second was indeed epic, with producer Dave Jerden recalling that to fully wrap his head around the song, "on *Three Days*- first of all, when I work on songs like that, that are long, in order to keep them from turning into jams, what I do is chart everything out. What I basically make is a score, like what an orchestra would have. At every point, there should be always focus going on, and set ups for the next bit, and resolves from the bit that came before. Its like working out a regular symphonic piece, and so I chart it all out, and then we rehearse it. And I keep an eye to the overdubs, to make sure there's always interest going on, and the feel of the song as its happening, otherwise it would just turn into a jam."

As the band crafted the multi-layers of effects that decorated the song, guitarist Dave Navarro recalled to Boss.com that "in the early Jane's Addiction days, Perry used to use a Jazz Chorus on '*Three Days*' - one of our songs. He'd play rhythm guitar on it through the JC-120, and it always had that classic tone. I'll tell you, that thing was louder than any other instrument in the rest of the band combined. It just cuts through anything." He added of the solo on '*Three Days*' in a conversation with Guitar Player that "I generally go into the studio not knowing what I'm going to do, though I know the basic song. I throw down a bunch of stuff. If it works, great; if not, scratch it. We do the basic tracks, all four of us live, then I do a rhythm part to double or match the basic. After that if I hear a space that can use something, I put it in. If I don't like it, I try something else. But I don't spend too much time--the solo on '*Three Days*' was a first take, the rough track. Anyone the least bit creative could spend forever in the studio, and I don't want to take our budget out the window. We pay a lot of attention to tones and sounds. When I introduce a sound, I like to give your ear something new."

Jerden faced the additional challenge of navigating through the band's personal acrimony in the course of capturing the song on tape, recalling that "on the first record, they all played together in the studio while we tracked. On the second record, Dave Navarro was on Methadone, and couldn't come in till later, and Eric and Perry weren't getting along at that point, so it was, for personal reasons, hard to get them in together. When I started *Ritual*, Perry didn't show up for 3 weeks, and so I stopped production, and then we halted production for about 5 months before we started up again, cause Perry was using Heroine and just couldn't show up. The only song I really got them together on was *'Three Days.'* " Underscoring just how significant an occasion it was for the band to be playing live together again, Janes' wound up tracking what became- quite literally- the song's money take during what became a live mini-concert before Warner Bros. head A&R executives- and Jane's Addiction's biggest believers and benefactors in the form of the extravagant $500,000 recording budget Farrell had been given to finance his masterpiece.

Sharing his recollection of what he considered "an honest representation of Jane's Addiction in the studio at their best," producer Dave Jerden recalled that the night the band recorded "the actual take that wound up on the album, we went into the studio, ran it down once, and then- just as we were getting ready to record it- Roberta Peterson and Steve Baker from Warner Bros., their A&R people showed up, and they played it for them, and everything you hear there we kept. We filled in a couple things, but mainly that was the performance they played with. The other songs were put together, doing the drums first, etc- but that was the whole band playing, and that's a real honest representation of Jane's Addiction in the studio, at their best, doing a whole song. *'Three Days'* was a highlight, a great performance." Engineer Ronnie Champagne added his memory of the night that "with the A&R people were in the studio sitting in the control room as the audience, and that night was like a little mini-concert. That was the most killer thing I'd ever seen, and it was our last-ditch effort to get the song done. We already had the other piece in the computer, so all we had to do was tie it all together, and just needed that really magical live performance, and I think we kept every bit of what we tracked. It was great because we'd worked so hard to get to that point, because Perry had the head of A&R in that audience, and made them total believers because prior thereto, there was pressure from the record company to make it super-special, but the A&R people were enamored by and in awe of Perry, and knew what he was about and how cool his stuff was. They were down for it."

Once the band had tracked their aforementioned money take, engineer Ronnie Champagne recalled from a technical standpoint they still weren't over the goal line yet. During the editing process that followed in the course of assembling all the pieces and parts of the sonic opus Perry had envisioned in his head, the engineer quipped that "we got into Midi-hell with a lot of this overdubbing happened in the second stage of recording, after we'd gotten the rock songs done and Perry was happy with them, this all of a sudden became a mini-opera. Once we started working with the keyboards on *'Three Days'* and *'Then She Did'*, and using the computer for the drums, so for instance, with the drums on *'3 Days'* and *'Then She Said'*, because we had Midi-triggers on the drums, which again is hell because we had to figure out ways to make it all work depending on... Steve is a very dynamic player, so we had a lot to work with, and had to get really hard hits and really soft hits and try to get it all into the computer. This is the age of old, square table-top MACs, 7800 series, like $4000 for that? Are you kidding me? It was a whole different era from Protools, so we were actually recording Steven's performances into a sequencer so we could straighten it out. We had a problem with tempo on both those songs, and had tried everything. We probably spent 10 days on those two pieces easily, and were doing all the old tricks- splicing things together- and we finally decided to go the Midi-route. So parts of the songs sound almost robotic, because while its still Steve's drums being played, they're being played off a sequencer."

To assist in navigating the latter technical maze, Champagne shared that they recruited "John Philip Shenale, who had a whole rack of stuff and did soundtrack stuff around town , and we worked with him for a couple days getting trippy noises, trying to get away from real standard-sounding keyboard noises. So for instance, on *Three Days*, he would give me a stereo-pair from his mixer, but with probably 8 modules coming out at once. Another guy we worked with was Geoff Stradling, those were our main go-to tech guys on the record. These parts were all tracked very quickly, so basically we'd say 'Here's the part, now let's add sounds to it till we think its done and it mixes with the track properly,' because adding parts to these kind of tracks, you have to play along with it, because you don't want it to overtake the track or pull the track into a direction it shouldn't go. The problem with most keyboards is that they all have such an identifiable sound to them, and we were trying to bury them really creatively within the mix of the song to get what Perry was hearing. Again, Perry would sit there and approve sounds as they went down too, and being an oral guy, he would sing the parts to John and Geoff as he heard them in his head, describing them with his voice, really complicated stuff. So for instance, if something had triples, he would sing it, and the guys we were working with were all ear guys, so they instantly could play what Perry would sing to them. Perry was the bottom line on all of that, because whenever it came time where we needed an answer on something, it was 'Just ask Perry,' and he'd have it."

In other creative instances, the engineer quipped that what fans wound up hearing on the finished album amounted to what was "definitely an element of happy accidents, because we didn't know what would happen ahead of trying some of the ideas we did, but we pulled it off in the end. I remember we had this bloody, nasty pile of gear in the middle of the room that was just computer hell trying to make all this stuff work. You've never seen a half dozen guys standing around, it was like the adage of men standing around looking at a car, scratching their chins, going 'Did you check the air in the tires,' it was days and days of that. Because we'd never seen this shit before, so everyone was adding in their 2 cents, getting frustrated, but we got through it somehow. Our group think was: what can we do with the technology at hand, and because of some of the things we were trying, we were asking ourselves, 'If this is so difficult, I wonder if anyone's actually done it before?' It was a challenge at times to marry the ideas Perry heard in his head with the available technology at that time, and the results were groundbreaking as far as I was concerned."

Critics were equally as enamored with *'3 Days'* sister *'Then She Did...'*, with Billboard complimenting the fact that "few (if any) alt-rock bands have composed a pair of epics that totaled nearly 20 minutes, let alone put them back to back for full dramatic effect." A deeply personal ode both to his former love Xiola and departed mother, Perry shared with a live audience of the song's muse that "this is a song about someone who I really loved and she died," adding in an interview with Raygun of his mother's own passing that "she died of a broken heart, that's what drove her to suicide... and we kids are all heartbroken. We missed out on a mother.... Nothing came of it, so I came to the conclusion: Why throw your life away? Why throw your life into the flame? Your life is the one thing you have to fight with, why give it up? I have never found anything big enough to give up my life to, especially if it was something that I hated or bothered me. The last thing I would give is my life. If I don't life something, I don't give it my time. I won't give it my life."

Guitarist Dave Navarro was moved enough by Perry's inspiration to share with Guitar Player that "*Then She Did...*' is my favorite track on the latest album," adding in another conversation with Jane's Xine about the deeper meaning of the song for him that it was so profound, "to try to tell you why would be like trying to tell you everything that has ever happened to me. Let's just say that for me, it captures most of the feelings I feel on a daily basis, both musically and emotionally. Also, that was a very special song for Perry and I... we used to look at each other when we were about to play it, and say, 'Let's do this one for our Moms.' Musically, in the course of crafting his guitar tracks for the album, because of that aforementioned respect, Navarro recalled to Guitar Player that, because "what Perry's singing about is beautiful, I didn't want to step on anything." To accomplish that, the guitarist shared with journalist Gary Graff that "I learned how to play guitar to serve the song rather than to serve myself," adding that in composing his solos, he embraced "the concept of letting the music breathe, as opposed to cramming it up with notes." Elaborating even more candidly to Guitar World on why he felt so firmly the song didn't "need a guitar solo," Navarro recalled that "the rest of the guys wanted me to do one and I said no. Lyrically, the song is beautiful and emotional, and it's got a very airy, open, moody tune. If I put a guitar solo in there, it would totally cheese it up."

While the band kept the song solo-free to maintain what Navarro heard as "a breathy kind of musical vibe," he did add touches of atmosphere throughout the song, explaining to Guitar Player that "on the breakdown of '*Then She Did...*', I improvised with my echo set on infinite repeats. You get this eerie feeling, but you can't really hear it. Its very quiet--I wanted you to feel uncomfortable and not know why." Bassist Eric Avery added his own musical recollection in a conversation with the same publication that "*Then She Did...*' started as a conscious idea to have a song that was stripped bare, without jazz fusion changes all over the place. We found that we could change the song with dynamics and very subtle changes without having to alter the chord progressions."

Quipping to a live audience that *'Obvious'* was about "nosey motherfuckers," engineer Ronnie Champagne recalled of singer Perry Farrell's idea during the song's recording to add a vocal track of taunting children that "here's almost exactly how it was put to me: Perry said, 'Imagine a bunch of kids dancing around, holding hands, singing *Fa La, Fa La, Fa La, Fa La La La La,*' and it had a very Yiddish feel about it. These were street sounds Perry used to hear as a kid growing up in Brooklyn, and that was pretty much all he had to say to me and I got it. Initially we toyed with the idea of a bunch of kids coming in to sing that, but Perry ended up doing it in the end." Of the "gypsy fiddles" that Rolling Stone Magazine hailed as among the album's "great bits" of aesthetic brilliance, engineer Ronnie Champagne recalled that "the violin part was an acoustic violin with a pick-up, I miced it with a 87 and ran it through a rig as well." During tracking for another of the album's violin-laden slower tracks, Dave Navarro shared of *'Of Course She Did'* in an interview with Practicing Musician that "we work off mistakes a lot. For instance, *'Of Course,'* which has violin in it and is very different for a rock band coming out of L.A. That was originally part of *'One Percent'* from the live indie album. It didn't work there. Now, some years down the line, it ended up being its own song." Drummer Steven Perkins added his recollection during recording that "I remember particularly *'Of Course'* being fantastically fun for me, because of the drum tracks. There's bells, chimes, timpanis, kick and snare, cymbal rolls. I mean, I had a great time. I did little finger bells and acted like a belly dancer for about two hours."

As moving in its own uniquely mysterious way as *'Jane Says'* had been on their first LP, Billboard commented of 'Ritual's *ballad* that "Jane's Addiction always had a knack for penning beautiful ballads with a ghostly edge, again proven by the album closer," the inspiration behind which Ronnie Champagne recalled "was an ode to Casey, I'm not sure we knew what was going to happen on that one before it was done, because tracking that involved some computers as well. We did some keyboard work with John Philip Shenale, but a lot of that stuff was actually organic sounds put through effects. For instance, on *'Classic Girl,'* the electric guitar has a really wiggly kind of sound, which was just modulation through the TC 2290 dynamic digital delay unit. We used that a lot for modulation, to get chorus and tremolo effects." The engineer added of the song's rhythmic evolution that "we recorded it live, but the end part of the song was originally all the way throughout the song, where the drum-driven part climaxed. It started out being rhythmically driven that way throughout, and eventually Perry decided to use that as an ending, we just muted it throughout the rest of the song."

Ironically, though the New York Times would observe in their review of the album that "softer tracks like *'Classic Girl'* show they can be melancholic too," for the band, the song was much more of an anthem about the moment, as famously captured in Farrell's conclusion near the song's own that "they may say 'Those were the days,' but for us, you know, these are the days." Elaborating years later in reflection on the deeper meaning of those lines among the band's own members, guitarist Dave Navarro that "when Perry sings, 'For us, these are the days,' I totally take a moment to look at where we are and what we're doing. That's a time in the set where I really feel gratitude. As many other projects as there are, this is the one thing that I feel has been my home and will be my home forever." The song resonated equally with rock fans across the nation's airwaves, propelling the song upon release in the summer of 1990 to eventually crack the Top 10 on Billboard's Modern Rock Singles Chart, peaking at # 5.

Trying to critically deconstruct the mystical musical riddle that was *Ritual De Lo Habitual*, Entertainment Weekly took a first shot by pointing out that "the music takes getting used to. It's far more unorthodox than anything on the group's first major-label album (1988's *Nothing's Shocking*). The songs come in great crashing waves, barely stopping for niceties like shapely melody or coherently changing chords. Toward the end, the waves slow down and the songs grow more tender, but it takes time to sort out their elements. The effect, sometimes, is as if careening speed metal had mated with rhapsodic mysticism, spinning off drunken bass lines, spiraling violins, even the sway of a bumpy waltz. The trick for a confused listener would be to fasten onto details like these, which can serve as musical buoys in an ocean of sound. Eventually the music starts to make sense, and Farrell's emotion ends up touching your heart."

Touching the hearts of hundreds of thousands of fans as the buzz from their underground movement continued to gain volume, drummer Steven Perkins in elaborating on that momentum in an interview with Ink 19, recounted the revolution as one where "I remember Jane's was making a scene in LA, then taking that LA scene and bringing it all around the country. It was influencing people, because there was a lot of passion to our music and what we were doing." Guitarist Dave Navarro added to Guitar Center.com his opinion that "I was so deeply rooted within the whole process that it was very difficult to feel any influence that it may or may not have had, I was just as absorbed in that band and the process and the touring and the record cycle at the point of Ritual De Lo Habitual that I had been at the point of the Triple X release. It gradually became larger stages but when we started playing, it always felt relatively similar and comfortable. It wasn't until much later that I realized that there was any impact whatsoever. I knew there was impact and I knew people liked us but I didn't understand that it was important, at the time."

Navarro - in an interview years later with Guitar Center.com- would recall feeling proudest of Ritual De Lo Habitual as a musical statement because "it moves me the most, artistically and sonically. All four of us were on top of our game, as musicians and creatively. Perry, in particularly, shines in a way that I hadn't heard before; that record just highlights all four of us the best. Its my favorite." Agreeing, Billboard Magazine pointed out in its review of the album that "while its predecessor, 1988's *Nothing's Shocking*, served as a fine introduction to the group, *Ritual de lo Habitual* proved to be even more daring," with Entertainment Weekly deeming the album to be "difficult, yearning, eruptive rock" that Stereo Magazine concluded listening to was "not a passive experience!" In measuring the universal impact of '*Ritual De Lo Habitual*,' we can begin by Billboard Magazine that the album "served as Jane's Addiction's breakthrough to the mainstream (going gold and reaching the Top 20)," as well as topping lists including Rolling Stone

Magazine's 'Essential Recordings of the 90s,' Q Magazine's 'Best Albums of the 1990s,' # 3 on the Village Voice's Top Album of the Year list, and # 3 on Spin Magazine's Top Albums of the Year, with the latter publication concluding in 2009 that "years later, it remains one of alt-rock's finest moments."

"Jane's Addiction's music is itself a product of the fragmentation and cultural overload that Mr. Farrell wants Lollapalooza to mirror." - The New York Times, 1991

"Lollapalooza...a slang word for something or someone striking or unusual." - Seattle Post-Intelligencer

Part 5: Parting Ways & the birth of Lollapalooza

In what would be the final year of Jane's Addiction's first age of reign over alternative rock, during which the world would witness the birth of alternative rock's very own traveling festival in the form of the Perry Farrell-brainchild Lollapalooza, the singer also coined the term 'Alternative Nation'- arguably to give a name to Jane's generation, one that the Los Angeles Times in its 1991 review of the festival observed was hungry "for a time when music had more integrity and daring and when there was a sense of commitment in the audience," further commenting that "the tour delivered everything it advertised...bands of alternative pop-rock shadings--from a touch of punk to a dash of metal to a tad of rap to a streak of industrial *Angst* --all woven together in an old-fashioned festival setting." The New York Times, for its own part, would note of the Festival that "there may be other, bigger-grossing tours, but for fans disaffected with routine concerts, nothing can rival the sense of expectation and event that Lollapalooza has aroused...There's no contest: This summer's biggest tour is the aptly titled Lollapalooza."

In between tour dates the band was sharing with founding gangster rapper Ice T, the emcee joined the band in the studio for a collaborative cover of Sly and the Family Stone's fittingly-controversial '*Don't Call Me Nigger Whitey.*' As famously captured on film in Perry Farrell's Gift, the performance was one that Ice T himself recalled came about after "Ernie-C, the guitarist from Body Count, had hooked up with Perry. He said, 'Yo, Perry wants to meet you.' I met him and he said, 'I'm trying to do this Sly Stone song, '*Don't Call Me Nigger, Whitey.*' You know it?' I said 'Yeah, I'm with it.' He said, 'Well, we got the cameras right here, man.' We actually shot that film of us singing that for Gift that first day. We just knocked it out." Of the aforementioned *Gift*, Perry recalled in an interview with the New York Times that "I told Warner Brothers I'd give them five videos if they gave me $125,000 to make a movie. And I went to Mexico and made a film. So basically I got Warners to pay for my vacation. Mexico is wild. The people are hot-blooded, the weather is hot, the food is hot. The art is great, too."

During this final burst of Janes-related creativity, the band also contributed a dreamy version of '*Ripple*' to a Grateful Dead Tribute album, '*Dedicated: A Tribute to the Grateful Dead,*' that also featured performances from Elvis Costello, Susan Vega, Dwight Yoakam, The Indigo Girls, the Cowboy Junkies, Lyle Lovett, Midnight Oil, Bruce Hornsby, and Los Lobos. Of the band's decision to record '*Ripple,*' guitarist Dave Navarro recalled in an interview with Guitar Player of the band's expectedly unique take on the song that "it sounds like Love and Rockets meets Sonic Youth with tribal drums, a repetitive bass line, and lots of grunge guitar. There are effected single notes soaring over the top with no direction. But Perry definitely sings the original melody. And there's something Deadheads might notice: at the end, we go into another Dead song, '*The Other One,*' and I through in a riff from Jerry Garcia's '*The Bird Song.*' It's a tribute to the Dead--I really like how they mix all their songs together live."

Announcing in the same time as he had the launch of Lollapalooza that he would be bringing Jane's Addiction to an official halt as a band following the tour's completion, the news came as a shock to fans of a band who had warned their listeners from the outset to be *shocked by nothing.* The New York Times most eloquently commented at the time on Perry's decision to break up the band and its potential impact that "Mr. Farrell's decision to end Jane's Addiction may confound the group's fans. The band is on the verge not just of major commercial success, but of becoming a countercultural icon for a disenfranchised generation. The singer is adamant, however, that his future musical projects will not take place under the name Jane's Addiction. The group is, however, going out in a blaze of glory. Lollapalooza is a boon for the twentysomething generation, a happening that may instill pride in teen-agers who have grown up under the shadow of rock's mythic past."

While drummer Steven Perkins confirmed the band's members were indeed still very eager to make new music for their fans, he recalled to Modern Drummer feeling at the time that- as far as Jane's Addiction was concerned- at the end of the day, "we wanted to move on, and we got locked into something we didn't want to get locked into--it just felt spent. Jane's kind of went full circle, to where if we went back into the studio, we would have tried to make a Jane's record--like, 'What would Jane's Addiction write?' --as opposed to what' really coming out of us. With this band, we want to make this record, put it aside, and make another record; just keep going like that. We've got a studio at my house now, so we can rehearse and write songs any time we want to and just push the record button any time anything new comes up. We don't want to depend on any set of songs to get us through our career. We want to create songs and move
on...Going back into the studio with Jane's just didn't feel right."

Publicly, at the time, Perry Farrell spun the announcement as a decision by the band to "go out on top" without the "safety net of Jane's Addiction," elaborating more in-deathly to another interview that "just playing with Jane's forever would be like listening to the same radio station for the rest of my life. My intention was never for us to just keep getting bigger and bigger, anyway. What people have to expect from me is not to expect anything." Drummer Steve Perkins added to Modern

Drummer his memory that "there were a number of reasons why we put an end to Jane's Addiction, and Perry is the one who first brought it up. It's kind of like having a relationship with your girlfriend that's gone bad. You're not getting along, you still love each other, and someone's got to say it's time to take a break. With Jane's, it was like, 'Well, we've done everything we can with each other. Let's find some other people.' "

Personally, he would share years later with a journalist that "we weren't getting along to the point that nobody was listening to musical ideas. If I said, 'Hey man, let's try being adventurous here and putting, say, a flange on this instrument,' if you're not friends, you don't listen to me. You tend to block out any suggestions. Suggestions grounded in love are always accepted." Perkins added of the personal inner-band tensions at the time that "musically we weren't finished, but personality-wise we were. We couldn't go past a certain point because we had personal problems. Sometimes those can be worked out, but there was this negative seed, where we couldn't make positive music anymore."

Elaborating in an interview with Guitar Center.com on the band's anti-climatic ending, Navarro recalled that while it wasn't unceremonious- in context of the band's final Hawaii show together live- "I just know that after the Lollapalooza tour we were exhausted from the experience. There wasn't really a day when we said we were breaking up, it just felt like we ended the tour and the album cycle and we just never did anything again until years later. I know that Perry wasn't excited about going back and I know that I wasn't, and I know that Eric and Stephen weren't either. I don't think it was even communicated, I think it was just a mutual understanding. I don't remember having a band meeting and saying 'This is over.' I think we all just stopped making (phone calls). I think that was cool because it lent itself to the option of reforming at some point, because there never really was, as far as I can recall, any heated problem to speak of."

"*Deconstruction* is about distinctive individual voices and sounds. What we've done is to say, 'This is what alternative music is.' " - Eric Avery

"They were kind of a strange bunch, and had this really ambitious idea for
Deconstruction." - Engineer Matthew Ellard

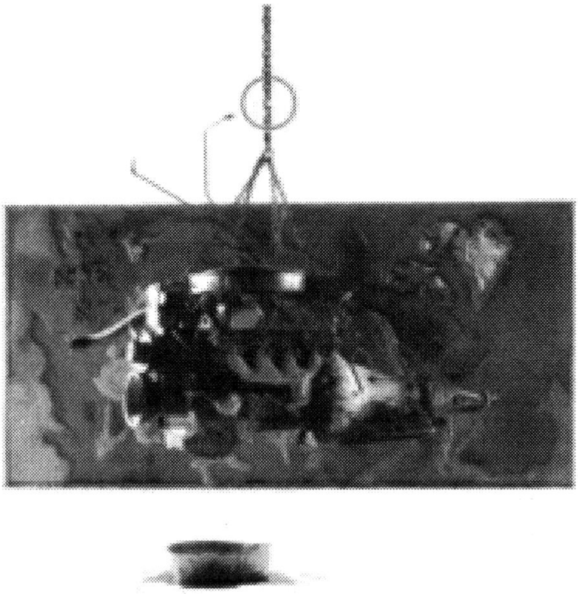

Part 6 : Deconstruction

Deconstruction has always proven something of a reviewer's enigma among rock critics, and a no man's land for many - who refused to directly insult the record they all wanted to be Jane's next. The same had been true for Porno for Pyros- take Entertainment Weekly's observation that compared to Jane's, "PFP...doesn't sound quite so exotic." Deconstruction, in the course of its release, took on the unfortunate burden of satisfying what Billboard Magazine noted as "the faithful (that)...were waiting forever for whatever the two would create next." The experiment had its invariable fans, with Guitar Player Magazine noting in its eventual review of the album that it "album blends samples and drum machines with live drums, pastes raw, tight grooves into elliptical arrangements, and exudes a cool, jaded-poet vibe courtesy of Eric's half-spoken, Iggy Pop-cum-Leonard Cohen-ish vocals. And it, uh, rocks."

Still, the album suffered from two great handicaps, one being what Billboard gently pointed out was a lack of a proper lead vocalist, noting that "Avery handles the majority of singing, and while he wisely doesn't try to create a knockoff of the patented Farrell whine and howl, his often staccato speak-singing isn't always the best of substitutes." As well, the band in the end suffered musically from the fact that Navarro left the project before its completion to join the Red Hot Chili Peppers. Still, at its outset, Deconstruction seemed like the perfect territory for the pair to explore, with bassist/vocalist Eric Avery recalling in an American Recordings press interview that "Deconstruction applied to where I was at the time...Shortly after the last Jane's Addiction concert in Hawaii, I rented a house in Big Sur. I ostensibly went up there to just detoxify from the whole Jane's Addiction experience. While I was in Big Sur, I spent a certain amount of time every day writing. It was really a discipline because if I didn't do it one day, I really felt like I was sloughing off. The nice surprise was that as I started to think about what I wanted to do, I got excited again...(Then Dave) began to write songs, not paying attention to what was being put out as far as the alternate of sound." Navarro added of the pair's decision to team up in the studio that "Jane's Addiction ended and we just got together and started playing music. Eric and I had wanted to do something on our own, somewhat removed from the whole Hollywood-L.A. band thing, and just do something for ourselves."

Navarro added in the same interview that as the pair dove headlong into pre-production, "everything was fair game as far as we were concerned. That was the whole point--to take elements of different types of sound and music, and put them all together, even if they didn't necessarily fit in. Eric had gone up to Big Sur by himself and had written a few things. At the time, I was getting my life together and writing a few things on my own. He came back, we had time, and we just basically started working on my 8-track in my apartment." As they headed toward the start date for recording, the guitarist refining the album's songs that "the creative process involved trying different things on 8-tracks and cramming them together. There was no method, there was no formula. Every song was its own thing. We just threw everything in a pot and discovered what tasted good. We wanted songs that weren't necessarily verse-chorus-verse-chorus-guitar solo-outro...We're not doing the verse-chorus-verse-chorus-bridge-solo-out thing...We're putting together elements of music that have nothing to do with one another, branching into areas we know nothing about, and combining them with things we do know something about...We didn't want standard rock songs, we wanted to be more experimental. I think we did that."

Expanding on the inspiration behind some of the album's specific tracks, beginning with *'L.A. Song,'* bassist/singer Eric Avery shared in an American Recordings press interview that "I felt the prognosis on my musical career was looking bleak because I had spent so much time with it being a business. I had made a joy a duty, a great phrase that I got from a friend's mother. I felt finished about making rock music. I was also simultaneously disillusioned about the whole alternative music scene, and I still feel that way. In the process of starting to think about it and talk about it, I started to get excited. I wasn't interested in making rock music per se any more. But then I began to think that it might be interesting to tinker around with song writing structure, not doing verses and choruses and things like that. That's when my interest was piqued about making guitar music, the idea of using loops and putting together parts like David Salle paintings, putting parts that don't work next to each other and seeing if a new relationship happens between them. This process lead up to *'L.A. Song.'* The first and second parts of *'L.A. Song'* have no real connection, but the fact we put them together does make sense because we allow them to exist side by side." Dave Navarro added that the song "captures what L.A. is about for us. It's a day in the life of L.A. Listening to it takes you through morning, noon, rush hour, evening."

Continuing, Avery in the same interview said of *'Big Sur'* that "I was just thinking about my travels up and down the coast during the making of this record and how much of a sense of place there is. I mean before we changed the name, there were three places named L.A., *Big Sur*, and San Francisco. But I was just thinking about how so often that's how David, Michael and I communicated to each other during the creative process. We would say 'It's like *Big Sur*,' and that's how we named it '*Big Sur*.' Because actually so much of what I'm talking about was in the desert and not actually from *Big Sur*. But I kept saying the first two verses should be like being in the city and then the middle part should be like you're driving up the coast and then the end should be that you arrive in '*Big Sur*'." A bit of a corporate protest anthem, Avery recalled of '*Get At 'Em*' that it "was the first song that I wrote, so it represented a lot of pent-up stuff. It seemed to build and build, and feel like 'too many heart beats a minute.' That was such a catharsis. At the time I had just come off being a commodity because we got so big in Jane's Addiction."

Heading into Cherokee Studios to record the album, engineer Matthew Ellard recalled at the time that "I was the chief engineer at Cherokee Studios, and Ronnie came in to set everything up, and ask me to be involved because I was so familiar with the place. The album was recorded in several rooms, it wasn't all done in one room." Engineer Ronnie Champagne's first concern where the album was concerned came with perfecting the drum sound, sharing to that end that "the nice thing about having a big budget is: before I even took Dcon into the studio, I decided to take some money and figure out what really are the best drums. I know everybody has their favorites, so I had every major drum maker bring me down their best kits, and I lined them all up on a sound stage, had the best guy in the business tune all the drums so there was no argument about that, did a shoot out and went through them all. And in the end came up with a set of drums that killed everything else, buried what people have been touting for ever as the bomb, and its not often that you get $ to toss away to do that. That doesn't happen anymore, but the drums we used on Decon are the greatest-sounding drums we ever worked with."

Elaborating on the duo's set-up for drum micing, fellow engineer Matthew Ellard "we recorded drums in the main room at Cherokee. We did it a little differently than usual. Off to the left of the tracking room there was what we called the 'Tile Room,' which used to be a mic locker, but then they took all the mics out, tiled it and turned it into this super bright bathroom sound. So we had the drums facing that from across the room at an angle, and I put a couple of microphones in the tile room and got this wonderful, super-bright natural reverb sound. Then I close-miced the kit, and we used a double-headed kick drum, and I took the front head off and put a couple of small mics inside- an RE 20 and another condenser mic- they had special wires that came out of a hole on the top of the drum, then we sealed the front head up so it became a sealed double-headed kick drum. I also had an 87 in front of the kick drum picking up the front head, and on the snared rum, I had a 57 and 451 on top, and underneath, a Senheisser 441.

Continuing, the engineer added that because "Cherokee had an amazing microphone collection, there were more than enough expensive microphones to put around all over the room. The overheads for the kit were U-67s and 421s on the top heads of the toms. The strange thing around the toms was we didn't put any bottom heads on the toms, and I set up 57s coming in where the bottom heads would be. So we had top and bottom mics. We had a bunch of room mics, including a couple of Tube 47s, a C-24 MS room mic that was out to the front and off to the right at an angle pointing between the toms at the snare drum, the rack and the floor tom. There was also a RCA 44 ribbon microphone above the overhead microphones, maybe a couple feet higher up pointing right over the top of the drum kit. There were also couple of microphones out in front of the drum kit a 6-8 feet back- an M47 and an M49- mono drums we used to call it. If you put those mics in the right position, you can use that microphone for everything."

As recording got underway, Ellard shared that "the basic tracks was Studio One, which is a beautiful big open-space room with areas of different ambience. The console was a custom console hand-built by the studio itself based off a Trident A Range design. Cherokee owned 7 Trident consoles, and eventually took one apart and started building their own version of it. Everything was recorded through Studer Tape Machines we rented, totally analog. This was before digital in the sense of Protools. The band was pretty well rehearsed when they came in. They had all the arrangements done. There were obviously a few songs we had more takes of than others, but I don't remember it being too complicated. We did some 2-inch tape editing to create tracks, because some of the songs we did in sections and then edited together. So we spent a while tracking the basics in Studio One, and after we did the basics, we moved into Studio Three, which contained an authentic Trident A-Range console, and spent most of the rest of our time there working on overdubs."

When attention turned to the album's extensive guitar overdubs, which Navarro in an interview with Guitar Player explained in context of his past work, still embodied "the heavier sound...but I don't think there's one straight power chord on this album. I'm doing a lot of clean single-note and melodic picking things. And I'm not so much playing regular rock guitar solos, although there are solo-type things. I would just rather play something that complements the music and the words, rather than stand in the spotlight. We're rearranging our thinking, so for us it's a stretch, but I don't think it will be for the listener." Describing a relatively relaxed recording atmosphere during overdubs, engineer Matthew Ellard recalled that "Dave would pretty much sit in a chair with his feet on the console and make it look like he was doing nothing while playing these ridiculously amazing riffs over and over and over again. On some of these songs, when we mixed them, there was 60 tracks of guitars. We had 2-24 tracks of tape filled up, and there were sometimes 3 or 4 things on each track. So it was huge and highly complex arrangement wise, these songs were, because there was a massive amount of information to deal with. We filled up an 84-channel SSL console, which is where we mixed in Studio Two, we used all the faders and a bunch of the small faders too, so there was A LOT of stuff going on. When we were mixing, we didn't have to recall the guitar settings that much, because they didn't change that much, other than we'd tweak the amp obviously, because a lot of the stuff was triple-and-quadruple tracked, most of the guitars."

Elaborating more in-depthly on Navarro's recording process, the engineer added that "we did all the guitar tracks in Studio Three. Dave's process when he's tracking was: he'd play the part, then he'd double it, triple it, then quadruple it, and build a wall of guitars like that. And his playing is so tight that it sounds like one massive guitar. There were two PRS guitars, because Dave was endorsed by Paul Reed Smith, so we used those for pretty much everything. I remember using a Telecaster for some of the cleaner tones, but it really wasn't one of those albums where you have to switch up guitars for every part, it changed from tweaking the amp and pedals he was using at the time. I'm still amazed to this day how easy he made it look, just relaxed knocking off these amazing parts in the control room."

The guitarist added in an interview with Guitar Player of the gear he utilized in the course of recording *Deconstruction* to that "I have two Boss Digital Delays in my pedalboard; one is for my regular delay settings...I have one setting that's an average delay time that seems to work in all the songs. In the studio I'll tweak the delay until I get the exact delay time that fits the track, but live I just try to find one setting that fits everything. And I usually prefer it if the time setting of the delay is nowhere near the time signature or tempo of the song. Since it doesn't really 'work,' it seems to make it a little more surreal, like your head doesn't know which thing to listen too. I also like to print the delay to tape; I don't like to add it in the mix. So one delay is for rhythm and solos, and one is just for that one special effect."

Expanding further, engineer Matthew Ellard added that while "some guitar players need a lot of amps and guitars to achieve differences in tone, Dave wasn't that kind of player. Dave used his PRS guitars, just one or two guitars, and a new prototype Bogner Ecstasy amplifier which I don't believe was for general sale at that point yet. We ran that through a Marshall 412 cabinet, and he basically had this huge board of some 30odd pedals, and got his differences in tone by jumping on the pedals. All the guitar recording was all done through a Neumann U-67 off Axis of one of the speakers, going through a Neve 1072 mic-pre EQ. Then occasionally, we'd put a Neve compressor in there to smooth a part out."

Where tracking Eric Avery's bass was concerned, the engineer recalled that "Eric recorded his parts in the control room as well, and he was playing a P Bass through an SVT and an 8x10 Marshall cabinet. I believe I miced him with a combo of a Phet 47 and a D-12." Of the record's extensive keyboard parts, Ellard added his recollection that, indeed, "there were a lot of sound samples and beats. Ronnie had a DJ17 keyboard, and he did most of the textures and extra bits, and was almost an extra member of the band in that sense, because he contributed a lot of musical ideas. He was very creative in a sense of adding stuff to the songs."

By the time Eric Avery was laying his vocal tracks, engineer Matthew Ellard shared that "Ronnie had moved on, by the time we got around to vocals, so I recorded those with Eric. We tracked in Studio 4, which housed an old Neve 8128 console, that's where we tracked most of the vocals." Of his vocal recording process, Avery shared in an American Recordings press interview that "at times, I've thought things like, 'Does Brian Ferry sing that way because that's the best he can do?' I always assume that these things are stylistic decisions people make. But in my case, most people wondered 'Why did Eric sing so low in a lot of the songs?' The answer is that's where I'm the most comfortable singing. In actuality, that's just the best that I can do." Rather than a vocal booth as former bandmate Perry Farrell had preferred, the engineer recalled that "Eric would sit in the control room, gave him a hand-held 414, and he would lay 15 or 16 tracks of vocals for each song, then I'd spend ages comping together a take. Me and Eric took a couple months to do vocals, which was like pulling teeth in many ways, because Eric's not a classically-skilled singer, but he had an idea. I remember there was a song that Dave sang on, and Gibby from the Butthole Surfers, which was an interesting day." With "over a year" passing during the course of recording *Deconstruction*, to keep track of the sonic chaos the band was stacking on tens by tens of tracks, as they headed toward mixing, engineer Ellard kept his head by turning to a tried and true ally of the analog engineer "when you're doing stuff like we were with reel-to-reel tape, the track sheet is the bible, so to speak, and I'm pretty anal when it comes to taking notes and keeping track of things- especially when you're working on a project as complex as that one."

Elaborating on why the project took as long as it did to complete, bassist/vocalist Eric Avery added in an American Recordings press interview following the completion of the project that "it really was like there were two processes going on during this time and that's part of the reason why it had to take as long as it did. It's interesting because what I had been apathetic about and ready to dismiss, I wound up a year and a half later fighting desperately to keep. This wasn't an easy process." Part of the challenge as the months of recording wore toward a year came with guitarist Dave Navarro's decision to leave the project prior to its completion to join the Red Hot Chili Peppers, with engineer Matthew Ellard candidly sharing his memory that "the only thing that really ruined the record was that Dave was lured away by the Red Hot Chili Peppers before we'd even finished." After leaving the project in a famous 1994 headline to join the Red Hot Chili Peppers, Navarro addressed the decision as one based foundationally on the fact that "it was never etched in stone that *Deconstruction* was a band we were going to do for a long time. I don't look at this as a band falling apart. I look at it like Eric and I just wanted to do different things. We did the record. We had a great time doing it, had a hard time doing it at times."

Delving further into the personal impact Navarro's decision had on him, bassist Eric Avery candidly shared during an American Recordings press interview that "the word deconstruction applied to where I was at the time and also was prophetic about where I was going to be a year and a half later. It represented the demise of Jane's Addiction, the final break between David (Navarro) and I, and really signifies that I really am no longer in Jane's Addiction. That part of my life is really in the past. The name *Deconstruction* fit instinctively without my knowing why. It seemed to dictate exactly what the experience was going to be about--not only in the relationship that I had with David, but how I made my music. It fits with deconstructive philosophy but the choice was totally unconscious, not contrived or manipulated."

When mixing commenced, which engineer Matthew Ellard recalled was primarily shepherded by he and Avery, sharing that "it was pretty much Eric's baby overall, and once Dave had started getting interest from the Chili Peppers camp, his input and interest started to wane. We mixed for three weeks in Studio Two at Cherokee on the SSL Eric was there every day when we were mixing, and usually would come in after Ronnie and I had everything set up and give his comments. We'd typically leave whatever song we were working on up overnight, and finish tweaking it the next day." Tackling the sheer complexity of the mass number of tracks, the engineer quipped that "I remember the album started to take a lot longer than expected to finish, there was just a lot of information on those reels of tape, and it took a while to get it all down."

By the time mixing wrapped and the album finally released on July 12th, 1994, Billboard reported that because *Deconstruction* "failed to support the release with a tour," the lack of promotion led "to the recording sinking from sight shortly after its release." Warning fans in advance that "this isn't a record for everybody," Navarro added in his American Recordings press interview that "some people will like it, some won't like it at all. We weren't aiming for mass appeal. We were aiming to get a lot of things within ourselves out in the open, which we accomplished. After Jane's Addiction, it was time to do something completely different, and we were a little selfish about it. We did more musically from a real cerebral point of view. *Deconstruction* is what it is. It was just a project Eric and I felt like we needed to do. I'm glad we did it. It helped me grow as a musician. I'm proud of a lot of the work on the album. It was a great learning process." Engineer Matthew Ellard added his own conclusion that "its a pretty amazing record when you sit down and listen to it, its an incredibly complex record. I thought the record was awesome when it was finished. I was from England, and the English don't make those kinds of records, so this was my first truly big American rock record I'd ever done, so it was a revelation to me. It was awesome, and it was epic and a really ambitious project to undertake."

"Perry went to one of the *Infectious Grooves* shows. I saw him out in the crowd, and he looked at me, and it was like this unspoken thing, like, 'Hey, we should be up here playing together.'...With Porno, everybody is so positive and likes each other. It's very refreshing. Another problem with Jane's was that we had to keep playing the same songs over and over because that's what people wanted to hear. We never got to write new songs." - Steven Perkins, 1994

Part 7: Porno for Pyros

Following Jane's Addiction's retirement, the alt-eyes of the rock world were squarely fixed on Perry Farrell's next move, which the singer admitted in an interview with rock journalist Dave Thompson that "its really hard to come back and do it again...People tend to judge you against your past...Are the players better? Is the music better? If the public turned around and said 'Eh?' Warner Brothers would bail on us like that!" Farrell's plan to keep his backers and believers entertained would come in the form of a provocatively named concept band, *Porno for*

Pyros, which Entertainment Weekly reported that "he wanted his next band, formed with ex-Jane's drummer Stephen Perkins, to be edgier and more experimental, worlds apart from the lumbering, Zeppelinesque swagger of Jane's Addiction."

Independently produced by Farrell and Matt Hyde- and inspired lyrically in large part by the L.A. riots- Perry commented of the muse that "(the riots) were damn sexy, weren't they? The excitement- I mean, let's face it, you can get a boner if someone slaps you in the face. Nine times out of Ten." Farrell's new band included Janes' drummer Steven Perkins, who commented to Modern Drummer of his decision to continue collaborating with Farrell that "I knew where my heart really was, and that was with Perry, making great music...Every time Perry and I played, I always felt something really strong with him. It's a love for music that we both share. We both loved playing live, which was the best part about being on tour--that hour on stage. But we both like making records, too. (Dave and Eric) loved music, but they didn't want to do it as much as I did. We all had a good time on stage, but everything that led to getting to that point each day was a mess. They didn't love the whole ordeal. They loved that one hour on stage, but they didn't like the other twenty-three hours...Perry and I know so much more about making music and making records, keeping the band together and doing the things you need to do to make it all work. We're just more mature as people and we've brought that to the other guys in Porno."

Rounded out by guitarist Peter DiStefano and bassist Martyn Le Noble, Perkins recalled in an interview with Modern Drummer that filling the latter position "was a tough one. We put an ad out in the L.A. Weekly for a bass player and got hundreds of calls on it. One night, we did an audition of about thirty guys, and the last one was a guy named Martyn Lenoble, who we ended up asking into the band. He's a really clever player from Amsterdam. European players have a little different approach than American rock 'n' rollers, so I found myself really listening to what he was doing and trying to play along with it. The thing about his parts is that they're not overwhelming or something that will take over the song. Perry, Peter, and I are more thrashers, whereas Mark is very controlled, and I had to learn how to take my thrash into his channel." The drummer further added of DiStefano's addition to the band that "he turned out to be a surfer buddy of Perry. They'd been surfing together for years, and Perry never even knew he played guitar! Meanwhile, we'd been auditioning guitar player after guitar player, and we met a lot of good players. But one day Peter picked up an acoustic and was just shredding, so Perry was like, 'I think we found our guitar player, who just happens to be my best surfer buddy!' "

Tracked at Crystal Studios in Hollywood, California over the summer of 1992, the band wrote as they recorded, with Perkins recalling to the same publication of that fluid, creative process that "the songs are coming very easily. It does take work, though, to make some of the complicated parts sound the way we heard them in our heads. But it's such a positive attitude that it just went by really quickly." Farrell added of the band's musical ambitions in an interview with rock journalist Dave Thompson that "Porno sounds a little like Jane's, but I think we've stepped it up." Talking more specifically about the band's songwriting process, which Perkins explained he and Farrell were aiming to be sonically opposite of their former band in terms of the minimalist approach they took this time out, the drummer shared that "Perry and I have gotten to the point where we're slicing off all the fat. Let's get trim and make the song. We thought, 'This is just bass, drums, guitar, and vocals. Should we produce it?' But why? If it's a good song, let people hear it as it is. With Jane's, the songs were great, but we were new in the studio and tried to tinker with little toys to spice things up. But Porno is bare bones, just the five musicians and that's it."

Creating a sound that Entertainment Weekly excitedly described as "grinding wah-wah guitars and clanky, trash-can-style drumming heighten the creepy-crawly atmosphere. Unlike too many pat alternative records, this record sounds like one of those amusement-park tunnel rides where you never know what's around the next corner." The New York Times, meanwhile, took admiring note of the collection of eclectic "songs (that)...jump from drifting ballad to wah-wah funk to blaring power chords, from bluesy rock to Perkins's hard-rock version of Latin rhythms." Perkins, chief musical creator of those rhythms, speaking on his compositional approach to writing the album's drum parts in a conversation with Modern Drummer, explained that "there are some parts where there are sparse, easy guitar strums with busy drums, like this song. I'm using my bongos a lot as part of the basic rhythm. I've got one crash cymbal, a couple of drums, and that's all I need. I just want to play the part and not fade off into something else." Continuing in an interview with Guitar Center.com that "my intention in Porno was to get away from the trap kit and incorporate more hand-helds in my drum set, making it more of a hybrid. I felt that the guitar riffs in Jane's kind of led the way, but with Porno I wanted the drum rhythms to lead the way. With the bongos in front of me instead of a kick, snare and hat, it became more percussive, more bubbly in a way, a little more interactive with the phrasing of the vocalist and less with the bass and guitar. So the Porno days really brought me to a new level of rhythm."

Quipping that "when I see Perry singing, I tell myself I have to be the baddest drummer--because that guy's the baddest singer, and I gotta make him happy," the drummer elaborated of the group's other members that "what makes this band; it's more like an ensemble. This band challenges me to be a better player technically. With the bongos, tombs, and snare going back and forth, it takes a lot more concentration to keep these intricate parts going. Some of the parts call for something jazzy, so I put pressure on myself to make them jazzy every time, because I know I can do it. So I press myself to loosen up, so I can pull of things--like a seven-stroke roll--when I need to. This new band has forced me to become more interested in the consistency of what I'm playing...I'm just trying to approach it all like a new instrument and it challenges me to come with something new...And the guys in the band pull that out of me."

Taking a more free-form songwriting approach than they had in Farrell's micro-manager days as Jane's co-producer, Perkins detailed a much more collaborative effort on the songs' instrumentals, offering a few examples where his drums actually played a pivotal musical role in the course of that compositional process, explaining that on "a couple of our songs don't have very much melody with the guitar or bass, so it's up to me to use toms, bongos, and timbales to make up a melody line. Instead of just rolling down the toms for a fill, I try to use them as part of a song. And I just bought a timpani that I set up to my left, and I'm tuning it to the song. That takes a little more work, but it's a fun drum...(With *'Pets'*), Perry's lyrics were about aliens coming down to Earth and realizing that we'd all make great pets who'd do anything for food...So I wanted to be the clock until that day came. Perry's lyrics triggered the idea, and the timbale allowed me to find that voice to work with the subject matter of the song...When I'm making my own parts, I want to go beyond that and make it my own thing, my own character. I want people to know that it sounds like Stephen Perkins." Offering a similar example with another of the album's tracks, *'Cursed Female,'* the drummer added in the same interview that "there...I did something I don't think I've ever done before, where I just play solid groove the whole time. The song needed a big drum beat that you didn't have to keep thinking about. It needed to be constant, hypnotizing--a beat to me that just feels like sex."

The project was kept so under wraps during tracking that by the time the band had wrapped, guitarist Peter Distifano revealed that "Warner Brothers didn't even know we were recording. We handed them a record and they were like *'wow.'* " Critics shared a similar sentiment, with the New York Times introducing the world in their review of the album to a "volatile, turbulent music (that)...scrabbles at emotions that rock rarely touches," while Entertainment Weekly boldly declared that while "Jane's Addiction may have hinted at the excess and ennui of a city and a generation...Porno for Pyros truly brings it all home; the result is the most compelling album Farrell has ever made."

Elaborating more generally on where the band fit into the mainstream alternative rock generation Farrell and Perkins had played such a pivotal role in shaping over the past decade, the magazine asserted that "Porno for Pyros couldn't have appeared at a better moment- a time when...alternative rock doesn't seem very alternative anymore. Farrell is partly to blame for the situation: Jane's Addiction was an arena act by the time it disbanded, and Farrell himself co-organized the lucrative Lollapaloozas. On *Porno for Pyros*, he sounds as if he realizes what he hath wrought — and, in his own messianic way, is trying to reactivate the adventurous underground spirit that once defined the genre. Call it Jane's Withdrawal." Still, for those Jane's fans looking simply to continue the love affair they'd had with its members from record one, Spin Magazine reassured with its concluding observation that "the die-hard (Jane's Addiction) fan will fall instantly in love with this LP."

Debuting at # 3 on the Billboard Top 200 Album Chart and going quickly Gold and then Platinum off the strength of the single *'Pets,'* which peaked at # 1 on the Billboard Modern Rock Tracks chart, followed by *'Cursed Female,'* which peaked at # 3. Extensive touring followed the release, including high-profile headlining spots on the Festival circuit, including Woodstock, where the band performed before 300,000+ fans, and by 1995, Spin magazine had ranked Perry Farrell ninth on its 'Ten Artists That Matter Most 1985-1995' list, solidifying his living legend as alt-rock's most influential front man and visionary. Musically, three years would pass between PFP's first and second LPs, and by their sophomore outing, the respect the band had earned- both from those who were instant fans, and those who longed for more Jane's but eventually came around- was reflected in critics like the BBC, who praised the band as "criminally underrated," while RIP Magazine hailed the band as "ahead of its time," arguing they were perhaps even a little "too far out there." Equally as dazzled critics agreed upon hearing the new musical ground covered on *'Good God's Urge,'* as highlighted by the New York Times conclusion that the band's new recordings comprised "an up-to-date counterpart to the music Syd Barrett made after leaving Pink Floyd. It is weird, candid and minimal. Moments of nonsense and endearing simplicity are mixed with revelations best interpreted by a team of psychorearysts."

For the band, the process of recording their new album, as Spin Magazine reported, "was inspired by surfing trips to the Pacific Islands," and for the band, an extension of what drummer Steven Perkins recalled to Modern Drummer was an attitude "more like, 'Let's go to Mexico for two months and Tahiti for a week and Fiji for month. Let's enjoy this and write songs on the beach.' We went for a whole other approach, on purpose. That attitude also had an influence on our work ethic. You didn't see too many Porno shows, but we were having a great time. It was the complete opposite of what Jane's was, which was a beautiful thing; working out of a garage and writing all the songs and touring in the van. Porno was just about enjoying the tour and enjoying ourselves immediately. We took advantage of it and it was a lot of fun." Continuing in a conversation with Ink 19, Perkins added that as "we traveled to Tahiti, Fiji and Mexico, all these wonderful sports...we wrote the record that turned into *Good God's Urge*. *'Tahitian Moon,' 'Bali Eyes,'* all that stuff was written in those spots. It was a wonderful, great time." Those good times were shared by Farrell's longtime friends Daniel Ash, David J, and Kevin Haskins of Love and Rockets/Bauhaus on *'Porpoise Head'* and Flea of the Red Hot Chili Peppers and Perry and Steven's former bandmate Dave Navarro together on *'Freeway'*.

Recorded at the band's own Shangri-La Studios at Zuma Beach and The Record Plant in L.A., Perkins elaborated on the band's creative in-studio process by explaining it as a simple extension of the band's desire to "keep creating. I see Porno as evolving constantly. We're thinking of things all the time, like putting a marimba on my kit. Then I'd really be able to play a melody. Kick, snare with one hand, and melody with the other hand. It might be hard, impossible maybe, but why have a floor tom and not have something that plays actual melodies? I want to get to the point where I can make music completely with my kit. I've looked into electronics and I bought a couple of Roland padds. I use them once in a while, but I never want to use them for a drum sound. Why put a snare in a pad when you've already got a snare? I find that pads are good for practicing and good for the studio if you want to come up with a weird sound or noise. But I want to hear real drums, and it hurts me to hear samples." As with their debut LP, the drummer recalled that " we got our keyboard player/sound effects guy (Matt Hyde), who's also an engineer, to do the engineering for the record."

Released on May 28, 1996, *'Good God's Urge'* made at Top 20 entry on Billboards Top 200 Album Chart, with mesmerized Melody Maker of the album's psychedelic soundscapes that "these cocoon symphonies are strange and disturbing things," warning listeners that "perhaps the biggest mistake you could make with *'Good God's Urge'* is to try to understand it....Far better to abandon logic and let it wash over you," while Rolling Stone Magazine noted that "*GOOD GOD'S URGE* is...split into two moods that make alternate pleas for compassion and fury." Offering their assessment that the "tunes confidently blend weird improvisation with gorgeous melody," the highly impressed Mojo Magazine added its concluding observation that the combination gave "the album both depth and beauty."

"We now have a new sound, and for a musician, it's so exciting to play (the new stuff) and nail it live as good as you can do it in the studio. And then it grows even further live." - Perry Farrell to Mtv.com, 2003

Part 8: Strays

It seemed to everyone like the members of Jane's Addictions were all just going through the musical motions of Jane's in the intervening studio years between *Ritual De La Habitual* and *Strays*. As with every great band, no one cared about the personal reasons behind Jane's announcement in 2001 that they were reuniting for the *Jubilee* arena tour that served to introduce a new generation of fans to their catalog of alt-rock classics. Selling out Madison Square Garden within minutes of the show's announcement, the buzz created itself as the band burned through a series of late 2001 sold-out arena dates, warming up fans for the what initially was rumored to be a working album title of '*Hypersonic*.' Coming off the road, Perry Farrell shared with MTV in April of 2003 that "it was an interesting way to record because when we got back in the studio we were even more on fire."

Steering the album's sound in a more electronic direction than past albums, Farrell explained to MTV that "for the past five years I've been involved in electronic music and production, and I thought it would be great to lend that sound to Jane's Addiction. We started out with that premise, but it was like trying to hold back a rocket. It was impossible to keep the band from taking off around the electronic because the electronic is heartless and absolutely metric and we are living, breathing, gushing, pumping human beings. So we just went for it...With electronics, there's a chance that we can pull out some things that weren't available back then." In a further departure from the Farrell-dominated production of the past, the band happily and harmoniously handed over the reigns this time out to legendary art-rock producer Bob Ezrin, who perhaps most famously helmed production of Pink Floyd's seminal '*The Wall.*'

The singer commented in the same interview of Ezrin's induction into the fold that "Bob lent us his magic and we're so excited...There are things on there that we call 'moments' that will just sweep you away." Still, Farrell made sure to reassure the band's core contingent that "as far as the writing...we've made sure to keep it very spirited — in other words, all live. Now that we have our base — the real drums, the real guitars — now we can start to layer things with electronics." Guitarist Dave Navarro added that in an interview with the band's official website that "Bob has a unique and most welcomed perspective in terms of getting the very best out of us as creators and players. I think that the combined energies of Bob...and all of us in Jane's Addiction has made this time in the band's career the most comfortable and enjoyable it has ever been."

For his own part, after years out of the spotlight, Ezrin- who MTV.com praised for helping "Jane's Addiction craft gradual dynamic builds, sweeping sonic vistas and colossal climaxes" - couldn't have picked a more perfect comeback project, commenting for his own part of the collaboration in an interview with journalist Brendan Mullen, "my job on *Strays* was to bring a sort of commonality to the process and make everyone think it was a group effort again and not just a bunch of solo projects trying to be strung together." Elaborating more exclusively, Ezrin added of his production approach with a band as musically complex as Jane's Addiction that- as with the Wall- that he essentially became a 5th member of the band, explaining that "its very helpful as a producer to be both a musician and a writer at the same time, if you're going to go into the world of production. I know alot of people aren't, they're engineers, or they're musical but can't actually play or write, but I think its very important, if not the ability to actually play something as an illustration, or collaborate in the writing process, be knowledgeable enough about music to actually pull out a recording, if you can't do it yourself, pull out something you can point to- say 'You see that, you see that set of changes or that transition, that's the kind of change we need here', to keep pushing till its done. Being a musician and a writer and arranger, its for me always been a matter of just being really hands on, I work with the band."

After being out of one another's company in the studio for over a decade, Dave Navarro happily shared with MTV.com that "we have never been happier, freer and more unified," while drummer Steven Perkins added in a conversation with Ink 19 that the reunion was "an amazing thing, because we love each other and kind of deserve each other. When I listen to our music -- and I've been playing with Dave since I was fourteen and playing with Perry since I was eighteen, and I'm thirty-five now -- we're all just intertwined musically and we're friends. It's all there. It goes back so far that it's easy to do this together." Coming back to the table with their producer as the proverbial *5th Beatle* this time out, the band- according to critics like Entertainment Weekly- allowed "producer Bob Ezrin...(to) envelop them in a Parthenon of sound, with Farrell's frequently Bono-like vocals leaving vapor trails over Navarro's neo-Zep riffs and the rhythm section's air-locked grooves. This CD sounds large, as if it needs arenas to accommodate its sonic mass and density." Drummer Steve Perkins added in an interview with Ink 19 that from a band perspective that recording with Ezrin, "we had the best time with the guy. Bob is the shit! He's really good at capturing what everybody is good at playing, you know? He knows how to pull out what we all do best. He's also the greatest musician, and he understands songwriting and phrasing of the lyrics and the drum sounds, technique and all that stuff. You've got twenty or thirty years in the making of Bob Ezrin. Everybody's pushing off each other, with new friendships like Bob Ezrin and older friendships. We've captured what we know we do best."

Each masters of their musical domains, for Perkins- whose drum sound MTV.com praised as "precise and turbulent, setting the mood for various rhythmic excursions," - the drummer explained to Ink 19 that by this point in his career, "I know what makes Jane's bounce and sound tribal. When we did the record, I went right to that. It's like, 'I'm going to the toms for this part.' I'm going to exactly what Jane's Addiction is, but I'm doing it better because we can do it better now -- and we can record it even better. Like I say, if you're driving a Ferrari, make sure you drive fast. That's what we're doing. I know exactly what gets these songs going, to be the Jane's sound." Given what Popmatters.com described as "an opportunity to enjoy the spotlight," who further noted in their review that "his ferocious drumming leads the way," the drummer added in the same interview that in the course of compositionally creating the band's sonic beatscapes, "when the guys give me a song, when we're writing, and I set up my drumset completely different than I did on the last song, I sound like a different drummer. I have a lot of jobs to do. I have a pulse I have to keep -- so people can feel the pulse -- but I also have a job to follow everybody's theme and their little motif and melodies. If Perry says something real important, I'll go and chase his lyric for a while, then I'll go back to what Chris is playing, then I'll notice Dave's got this riff that's kind of standing out, and I'll follow him. So, I am orchestrating the drumbeat as I go. I'm not just playing a solid backbeat, but I am implying the back beat at all times. Implying there's a simple beat there, but playing around it and then definitely using the bass line, the guitar part, and the vocal part."

In helping Perkins capture that drum sound on tape, producer Bob Ezrin shared for his part that "the rule is in the hands, but, in terms of drums, also very much in tuning. If you have a very well tuned kit, musically tuned, where every drum is speaking, and speaking beautifully, you can put one mic up above them and one mic in front of the bass drum and make it sound good. You really need to sound there, one thing I encourage young producers and engineers to learn is how to tune a drum kit. Because most drummers don't know. And out here, they've created a whole industry of people who come to your studio and tune your drums for you. First they rent you a good sounding kit, then they tune it for you, and charge you a whole lot of money. So, one of the ways of getting the advantage of that without having to pay the price is learn how to tune your own drums."

Elaborating on his creative process this time out in the studio, Perkins shared with Ink 19 that "it all starts with being in the studio. I like to strip down for each tune and try something fresh, and then come back up with a new kit for each song. Taking that into an interpretation of the live show, I think it's important to have the basic four piece -- kick, snare, tom and a floor tom -- and from there I like to decorate. People think I have things placed in weird spots, but I'll always have a 10' or a 12' right in front of me and a 14' or a 16' as a floor. I'll have that as my basic (set up) and then I'll throw a bongo over there, a timbale here and an 8-inch on my right, a 12-inch on my left. To me, it's just a way to express myself on the instrument. I don't have to be a guitar player, where the strings have to be in the same place every time. I feel like there's a freedom to the drumset, there's a reason you can move things around. I take that to the extreme. Also, I like to play a tom like a ride cymbal, a bongo like a floor tom, and sometimes by just throwing it up there, it opens up things for me. I'll think, 'Wow, if I put a snare where the floor tom would be and the floor tom over there next to the hi-hat, what kind of beats I could come up with?' All of a sudden, I'm looking at these new beats that I would never really just happen to fall upon, unless I moved the drums around. Then I get used to it, I start playing that way, and it becomes my sound for the next six months with timbales and snare drums and ice bells. Then I'll think, okay, I've done that, I've really captured that frequency and I've written songs with those sounds. Now let's write some songs where I put the floor toms everywhere, and big 24-inch ride cymbals, and I'll just play big and...simple. I'll get into that for the next four months and write songs that way with the guys. That way, looking back, I've got a nice colorful spectrum of musical drum parts, different sounds, and different ideas. The drumkits themselves are forcing me to change and by me changing the drumkits... well, it's a friend of mine. I have to change it to make it change me. I want it to excite me, so, how do I excite myself with this drumkit? Well, I'll try something unusual. I'll put two bass drums up -- I'll actually be a double bass player for a while, with an 18" on my left and a 22" on my right. I'll see what I think of then."

When tracking the album's electronic drums, Perkins the same interview that "with electric drums, you don't even need to place drums; you have one pad and a nice drum brain and you can have a whole selection of drum sounds. I do like to have a couple of electric pads around me at all times in the studio. Sometimes you don't use them on a song -- it's not called for -- but here comes the bridge, and I'll find an 808 sound in the drum brain, and pop it on the bridge. Either people will look at me and go, 'What the fuck are you doing?' Or they'll go, 'Cool man, you're gonna do that? I'm gonna try something like this on the guitar.' And we'll just work off each other, but someone's got to throw something into the mix. So I start with a four-piece drum kit, and then just decorate around it."

Popmatters.com further noted in their stellar review of the LP that "Perkins' drumming is complemented by (bassist Chris) Chaney's studio expertise, making for a precise rhythmic foundation," Chaney himself explained in an interview with Drowned in Sound.com that joining and recording in the studio with Jane's Addiction was "the most gratifying because I wasn't so under the gun in terms of time. I've done a lot of records and a lot of sessions for other bands. Usually you're crunched for time. If you don't get it that minute or that hour, you don't get another shot at it. With Bob Ezrin, we were afforded the luxury of another day if we wanted to change something." Feeling that "Chris definitely stepped up to the plate" during the band's writing for the album, which was largely done during recording, the band's guitarist Dave Navarro added in a blog from the band's official website that the bassist "has been a key factor in helping us expand our creative vision and enthusiasm." Drummer Steven Perkins added with equal enthusiasm in his conversation with Ink 19 that "I feel great about Chris, because he's a brand new ingredient, and these old friendships are being sparked by his new friendship and the way he looks at it. Chris went to Berkley School of Music and he's got this whole other idea of theory and stuff that Dave and Perry and I take into consideration, but we don't know that much about it. I don't know much about music theory. Chris does and it's really cool to have that kind of angle. He's one of the band members, but his playing, his chops and his technique have nothing to do with the feel. The feel is all fat, round and groovy, but what's behind all that is really schooled. He's an amazing musician, to have all that together. He's played on many records also. He's the type of bass player that can learn sixteen songs for Michelle Branch, fly out and do a show as part of her band, then come home and finish the record with us. It's a great additive to Jane's as a band, because he's an inspiration for us."

Of his own collaborative compositional process with Chaney in the course of crafting the new album, the drummer in the same interview added that as he wrote with the band, "I focus on everybody and (start with) the bass line, I'll come up with a rhythm to play with the bass player. Then I'll stay with that rhythm. Then, here's the guitar part, and his rhythm's a little different, so don't forget to accent a couple of those ideas with Dave, while keeping the other rhythm going with Chris. And now, here's Perry, and he comes in and just dances on top of the whole thing. He doesn't really listen to the ones or the fours. He's just phrasing himself where he likes. He'll sing a long note, and he'll go over the piece, then come and sing with some short ones, real percussive, so I've got my eye on Dave and Chris, doing that, and there goes Perry. The most important thing is to never lose touch with the pulse that makes you shake your ass, basically. I think it's important to play the basic drum beat, when the song needs a lot of space, but sometimes I think the song needs to be a little more interactive and a little busier, and that's when I'll start going off a little. I think that's what you're hearing as more than one rhythm."

For as much as Perkins, Chaney and Farrell individually and collectively brought to the table, in the opinion of many of the album's listeners, including critics like Entertainment Weekly, "more than anything, '*Strays*' is Navarro's showcase. He's this record's fossil fuel -- its indispensable resource -- and '*Strays*' benefits from his imaginative downshifts and fanciful detours," while MTV.com added its own assessment that "Navarro plays with galvanic and artful intensity, contrasting evocative arpeggios with crashing riffs and ripping through furious solos with deft nonchalance." Explaining in an interview with Guitar One that " what happens (in the studio) is...I try to focus on a little bit of the technical, a little bit of the studio, and a little bit of the ethereal," the guitarist offered- in a conversation with Boss.com- the further insight into his creative process that "the truth of the matter is that I've been known to attempt to match speeds and tempo, but it never comes across as sounding live to me. So I pretty much dial it in by ear, and go with what feels best with the parts or solos that I'm playing. Sometimes I really like having the 'spill' being at different places than where the song is, and that kind of creates an ethereal quality that makes the guitar sound like it's coming from its own place. I'm not a purist. I don't necessarily need you to hear the pick against the string, or the bridge of my hand rubbing across the strings, you know? I want it to be slick and smooth, and sound like it's coming from outer space."

Quipping to Guitar Player Magazine that in contrast to earlier records, when "there were times when I'd play something kind of mediocre or something you'd heard before, and Perry would say, 'Try that again--but backwards.' I would never be able to literally do it backwards, but what I would come up with through thinking that way would be cool," this time around, he took more time for himself to map out what Popmatters.com deemed "electrifying fret work," explaining to Boss.com that "in the studio, I like to have an experimental day, where I can play with every effect imaginable at my disposal, and I just kinda pick and choose. I have a pretty good idea of what I want to lay down, and then I'll spend several hours just playing around. I'll sit back, listen to the tracks, and see what else I can tuck in there. I'm really into textures. And when it comes to amplification, frankly, I'll do the same thing."

Producer Bob Ezrin, in working with a guitarist as advanced as Navarro, agreed with the records' critics' assessments that "with a guitar sound, the rule is it comes from the fingers, everything else is secondary. If you got a player who can really play, he can make anything sound good. He can play it on a cardboard guitar though a pignose and make it sound like he's got a doublestack of Marshalls if you mic it properly. It starts there, it starts with the fingers, now often we don't have the luxury of working with great guitar players. Its very often we have to work with people who are, good, but don't necessarily have the magic fingers that somebody like Dave Gilmore or Jeff Beck would have, and then you need to augment what they're doing with attention to detail, what kind of guitar you want, each brand and model of guitar has a characteristic sound, matching with an appropriate amplifier, making sure you're micing it all correctly."

Elaborating a bit further on his expansive collection of gear utilized during the recording of Strays, Navarro shared with Boss.com that "in the studio, it's 'whatever I can get my hands on the better.' There's usually an arsenal of guitars, from old-school classics to brand-new BC Richs and everything in between: Strats. Les Pauls, SGs, and, of course, the Paul Reed Smiths. I use a multitude of different BOSS pedals, and I'll also go so far as to use some of the old-school stompboxes -- from the crappiest sounds I can find to the most modern and complex." With the result, Popmatters.com would conclude that "Navarro's dazzles listeners with...superb playing, and stamps the album with his distinctly heavy brand."

When attention turned to lead singer Perry Farrell's lead vocal tracks, which MTV.com would note were "filled with mystery and urgency," the singer shared the reality with fans in an interview with Ask.men that at times, "being in a studio is a day after day grind. The creation part is just crazy. You are unhappy with what you have and try to be a perfectionist." Bob Ezrin added that when working with a visionary as precise in his artistry as Farrell, his job as producer was to keep constantly in mind that "there are some laws of performance that one has to be conscious of, the most important thing is you want to put your vocal performer in an environment that will cause them to do their best work. It depends on what the performance requires. It if requires comfort and ease and soaring vocals, and joyful sound, you better make sure your singer is happy and comfortable. And most importantly, when you're making a record in the studio, the one thing that will inspire a singer more than anything else is being able to hear the sound of their record as they sing. What I mean by that is, giving them a mix, either on headphones or on speakers, for a singer to sing with, either one, you give a mix and make sure you have speaker or cans that sound good enough so that it sounds like the finished record in his head. And every time he opens his mouth he thinks he's hearing a hit single, that will inspire a person to perform more than anything else in the world. When you give him a really lousy mix, and the guitars are up here, and the drums disappear, and vocals are gone, if its a lousy mix for them to listen to or perform to, they will give you a lousy performance."

With Farrell, obviously the latter was avoided entirely, in part because Farrell's writing on the album's lyrics as always as impassioned as his performances in the studio. Beginning with the magic *'To Match the Sun'*, which the BBC observed "simply shimmers with an epic intensity," Farrell candidly shared of its inspiration to MTV.com that "it's about a man and a woman who can't be together at all times so they decide when they are apart they will watch the sun go down, and their hearts will start to beat together and that will be their time to be together...I want to tell you more but I am getting choked up." Elaborating, he added of a personal album favorite, *'Suffer Song,'* that the song was "about a tragic girl who had everything made as a young girl growing up. And then she had to get down with the people and suffer with them to fit in, as opposed to taking the fortune that was bestowed upon her from birth. And then she ended up doing tragic things with her life."

As the band wrapped recording on unbelievably only their third studio LP in 15 years, drummer Steve Perkins shared with Ink 19 of the finished product compared to the band's back catalog that "(the new LP) is way harder; twice as deep and dynamic and heavy. It ain't kinder and gentler; It's heavier and faster and more furious. We're pissed off! You can listen to 'Whores' and you can listen to *'Had a Dad'* or the end of *'Ted Just Admit it'* -- 'sex is violence!' -- all that. You can put it right next to what we've just done, and it's just fucking right there. It's just like, Uh! We knew, as Jane's Addiction, we could do anything we want, but if we're going to call it Jane's Addiction, we know we're driving a Porsche or Ferrari. Jane's Addiction is putting your finger on fast -- and not fast as far as tempo but fast as far as what we're doing. We're hypersonic!"

Though the band was clearly excited in the moment about the creative results of their blood, sweat and musical tears, looking back in hindsight years later lead singer Perry Farrell - in an interview with Rock

Sound- would admit that the process of letting go to allow such a collaborative environment "was difficult for me in that I had to give up more leadership...I thought, 'Maybe I should be more democratic. They've earned the right to have more opinions, I suppose. They've been in the game as long as I have.' So I was open to other people's musical ideas. I wasn't thrilled but so be it. Sometimes you have to bend. If there's only so much room you have to bend and make room. That's what I did." The results,

Debuting at # 4 on the Billboard Top 200 Album Chart upon release on , the album that Entertainment Weekly hailed as "the stuff of which comeback dreams are made of," fans snatched up 110,500 copies in first week sales, also propelling the band's first single *'Just Because'* to # 1 on the Modern Rock Tracks Chart. So much a fan of the latter hit, MTV.com concluded that *"Just Because* encapsulates the energy and positivity of the rest of the album, a joyous celebration of life peppered with pointers about how to make the world a better place without stalling the party." Of that record, the band were its biggest fans- ahead of critics- clearly feeling the music was as much a personal accomplishment as a professional one, as displayed in Perry Farrell's candid reflection to MTV.com that "I came up to California as a stray...I'm a Greyhound Kid. And then I ran into these guys (to form Jane's in 1984), and we got together for a short time and had an incredible time and an incredible journey. And then we all strayed off (in 1991). And then almost 13 years later, we strayed back together. And it feels great." Drummer Steven Perkins added in a conversation with Ink 19 his conclusion that on Strays, the band had grown by capturing "the energy of Jane's Addiction with the positive, electronic spark that was Perry's voice from the song *'Ocean Size.'* 'Three, Four!' Smash! That is right on, but it's also a new sound quality, sonically, and the progression of being ten years older, smarter, better on our instruments, and having all of the different stuff you can use at your fingertips in the studio now. All that shit goes into the new Jane's Addiction."

An instant lovefest ensued with critics worldwide like the BBC, who concluded that *Strays* was "a stupendous beauty, every track is an utter gem," adding their observation that "Jane's Addiction have never been constrained by the need to repeat themselves just to please less adventurous of critics." But pleased they were indeed, with Entertainment taking note of the band's "compelling chemistry" on an album that Popmatters.com asserted was "expertly crafted" while MTV celebrated the fact that the band had kept continuity between their past and current musical generations, noting that "musically, *Strays* blends the kinetic drama of the band's 1988 record, *Nothing's Shocking,* with the sonic exploration of their second disc, 1990's *Ritual de lo Habitual,* but does so cleanly and concisely, filtering grandiose themes into four-minute songs tailor-made for rock radio...In the end, the songs are fleshy and pulsing with life." Agreeing wholeheartedly, the Boston Globe added its upbeat report that "for Jane's Addiction fans, the good news is that 'Strays' - the band's first new album in 13 years - recaptures the sound that made the group MTV darlings."

Aside from the commercial aspect of their achievement, the BBC seemed excited for the band personally through its observation that "on *Strays,* Jane's Addiction really do sound like a band enjoying themselves again, doing whatever the hell they like, on their terms, and making some of the most exciting music around today...Jane's Addiction are most definitely back!" The legendary broadcasting network further advised its younger listeners/viewers/readers that "if you know what's good for you you'll run out and buy yourself a modern masterpiece right now." Ultimately, for band founder, lead singer and head conceptual visionary, Perry Farrell- reflecting back on the band's finally coming full circle with the musical movement they founded- explained in interview with the A.V. Club that "we came from post-punk, and we created the alternative nation. And it was very healthy for a long time. I don't know where radio is right now. Maybe they're looking for something new. That's why I'm saying, 'Let's create something. Let's put some enthusiasm into the sound.' There are lots of familiar elements to what I'm doing now, but it's like a child that comes from two different nationalities. It's just a beautiful new being."

"Convinced that electronica was the next bold step forward, so he absorbed the sounds and learned how to make it himself, crossing it with worldbeat and new age spirituality for his ambitious comeback record, *Song Yet to Be Sung" - Billboard Magazine*

"When it comes to Jane's Addiction I keep them separate because there are instruments and the lead instrument is a guitar...as much as you try to push it towards dance, they don't really like each other that much. We can do a little bit of electronic drumming, that works, but other than that I try to keep it more on the Pink Floyd and Led Zeppelin tip where it's being generated by the players themselves. When it comes to Jane's Addiction, it will remain what it is." - Perry Farrell, URB.com

Part 9 : Perry Farrell Goes Solo and holds a Satellite Party

As Porno for Pyros wound down into the later 1990s, lead singer Perry Farrell, as Time Magazine reported, "spent years learning how to program computers, spinning turntables as a club DJ and then applying these skills to create what he calls "sexy party jah music," producing in the process an album that Metroactive.com would hail as "a Magical Mystery Tour of electronica richly spiced with Middle Eastern sound...(containing) Farrell's best material since embracing Kabala and dance club culture." The Independant.co.uk celebrated the album for its stylistic diversity, noting that by "drawing on dub, electronica, and drum'n'bass textures, the record is a joyous if flawed work which Farrell's fans will recognize as a laudable attempt to keep innovating."

For the eclectic vocalist and visionary, that was precisely his sonic aim in crafting an album that he explained to MTV.com was to "look at this album as an evening, a concert...We love to hear great DJs, great records. We would love for it to be in a forest. We also want to hear people sing, play acoustic instruments and combine the two. At a certain part of the night, we're gonna all get really up and giddy, and we want to bounce around and hear some drumming." Elaborating in a conversation with Clear Sounds Magazine, Farrell added that "I made *Song Yet To Be Sung* purely as a listening disc, like if you're driving to the party or when you've got guests in your house...A lot of people don't necessarily like to listen to electronic music in their homes because they don't have the kind of electronic music that I've made along with my peers. Too often, the records are dark and grating, and there's not enough of a female sound. I wanted to make something happy."

Conceptually, the album's musical moods were inspired in by aforementioned broader concept of a Jubilee, which he explained to Clear Sounds Magazine meant "a jubilee for this time means a great, great party. It's the oldest kind of prophecy going, and it has to do with the redemption of man and of the Earth...I feel I have a Jubilee spirit now because I am aware of what it is, and it ignites something within...It's an intelligent way for everyone on earth to coexist with each other, where fights can't go on longer than 50 years. The next generation doesn't have the debt of people's feuds and monetary servitude." Elaborating on the historical roots of the album's theme word, the publication added that "this jubilant spirit of which Farrell speaks is based upon the ancient Jewish cycle of Jubilee described in the book of Leviticus. Occurring every

50 years, it is a yearlong celebration intended as a time of forgiveness, liberation, debt absolution, charity, and personal redemption. Joining the ever-growing list of celebrities embracing the Jewish branch of mysticism known as Kabbalah, Farrell's latest musical ventures merge his newfound spiritual awareness with his other recent discovery -- electronic music."

In crafting the rhythmic sounds capes that MTV.com likened to "a jubilant swirl of programmed dance beats," Perry added in the same interview that with the latter he'd sought to create "music that has feeling and is hitting chakras and healing us; music where the tribe and the gathering itself are important. It's not a bombardment; it's yummy and organic and has feeling...I like to use the tribal sounds because the most ancient sound is the one that is eternal. There's an earthiness there; it's the voice of the land. And to put it together with these modern electronic sounds is very representative of who we are today. It represents our Jubilee generation." Elaborating on the latter electronic muse as it translated to his own sound coming to life, Farrell painted a futuristic vision wherein "if visitors came, maybe not from another planet, but from a future dimension or the upper realms of heaven, would they have the power and ability to make sound with electronic instruments? Absolutely, and they would probably be unbelievable. I tried to imagine that when I was writing this album. For me, sound is like food...I love to go out and munch it up. I go to clubs and record stores ... otherwise I'd be starving. When I started to hear what these electronic composers were doing, it would be impossible to live the rest of my life and not take an adventure with these sounds."

Noting the sophistication of the record's musical soundscapes, Time Magazine quipped that "simple the album is not...Ambient pulsations and digital blips bubble alongside more familiar rock instrumentation on the CD, which also continues his fascination with swirling raga rhythms." Farrell- in revealing some of the derivative influences at play on the record- began by sharing with the Denver Post that, as DJs went, "my heroes are people like Derrick May, Sasha and John Digweed," adding in a conversation with the San Francisco Chronicle that "I love the subsonics and filters and delays...electronic music has a lot of positivity to it. That's where you're going to find the good, uplifting stuff. I feel enlightened souls put this music together."

Vocally, Perry applied the same vibe and energy in the studio, revealing to the Independent.co.uk that "I don't need that angry, pro-wrestler thing in my music any more. I still use strong sounds, but I try to make them reflect what's joyful, funny, deep, preposterous or... sexy, maybe. After that I start to filter things out," adding to Time Magazine that "I took my cues from Bob Marley, because his sounds are warm and organic and inspired. If the songs get too cerebral or wordy, you can't kick with them relaxing in a hammock." Delving into the lyrical inspiration behind some of the album's specific tracks, Farrell- beginning with the album's opening track, a collaboration with Jane's bandmates Dave Navarro and Steven Perkins- explained of 'Happy Birthday Jubilee' that "Jubilee is a party within a flame. The world is constantly at war with each other, and people are so numb that they fan the flames. But at the same time, we have to bring a celebration, and that's what it sounds like. It's about everyone showing up for the party." Of the intimately personal '*Our Son*,' inspired by the birth of first child Yobel, the singer/songwriter recalled to the Independent.co.uk that "I was with Yobel one day, and even though he was just a few months old, I noticed that he was responding to this giddy, happy Stephane Grappelli music. My eyes were opened. You don't have to go very far to see pain, sorrow and agony."

Still, in sum, the musical journey Perry took fans on in the course of '*Song Yet to Be Sung*' was a joyous one overall, and one he explained to Time Magazine he hoped translated to mean "a great, great party," adding to the same publication was an LP he took sole musical responsibility for as producer, explaining that "I've always titled projects as if they were a movie...This time I didn't want to share musical responsibility. It was simply mine." The results, critics would almost universally agree, was as unique as any recording endeavor he'd ever been a part of creating, with the Denver Post hailing the album as "an eclectic, loungy electronic work" before concluding that "Farrell has cultivated an original sound."

For all its electronica leanings, Metroactive.com was quick to note in its review of the LP that while "Farrell clearly intends *Song* to be more of a dance album than a rock one, and yet he hasn't lost his hard-rock edge," while the San Francisco Chronicle argued that one style begat the other in the context of Farrell's catalog, noting that "Farrell's interest in electronic dance music should come as no surprise to longtime fans who could detect a heavy rhythmic leaning in even his earliest work with Jane's Addiction," before concluding that the fusion was "simply a matter of time." Commenting on his ability to blend the styles so seamlessly in the course of the LP, Perry explained in a conversation with the Denver Post that it was a carefully plodded path wherein he stayed conscious of the fact that "I myself am particular about my rock, and I'm particular about my house music," before making the case that "there are ways you can break people who are all about rock into electronica. Breakbeats have a lot of rock and a lot of funk. Rock fans can digest and enjoy that." Regardless of the stylistic mixings at play on the record, Billboard ultimately concluded that "Farrell certainly has his own brand of mysticism, globe-spanning electronica, and he keeps his focus throughout the record, letting the moods change slowly with the flow of the rhythms. It's easily the most consistent record he's cut since *Ritual de lo Habitual*, and it has a generous spirit that's brand new to Farrell's music."

Expanding on his jubilant musical concept, in 2007 Perry struck out again on the solo path, this time with an impressive roster of collaborators, launching a Satellite Party that he explained to the Austinist conceptually was something that "initially I had thought to put together...(as) a room where people could hang out for a weekend that was like a space pajama party. I imagined that happening in the future where people would take commercial weekend flights into space. And, who knows, maybe they would do moon shots or something like that and hole up in a moon hotel. On the way to and from, they'd be floating in a satellite. So, I started writing the music to kind of go with that theme. When I wrote the music originally, it was going to be more house music and beats and things like that. Then, when I started laying lyrics to it, the lyrics began to tell a story, and I had the desire to add a rock band to it. We ended up actually laying over that a 30-piece orchestra. So, it was really a lot of fun to make the record, and it really did launch the project. I see this group touring for the next ten years. I want it to coincide with the changing of the world. I believe that there is going to be a massive overhaul, world change, in the next ten years. You almost won't recognize the world. I want to be there at the end of that ten years to celebrate all the good work that we've done."

Describing the foundations of his production concept and approach for the record- which he shared with the Acquarian Weekly he wrote much of on "my laptop. I've got the most badass laptop in the world," Farrell shared in a conversation with the AV Club that "the term I use is 'sedimentary rock,' because it was built in layers. Sedimentary layers of sound, beginning with electronics and subsonic sounds and programs, and moving through to the enthusiasm of rock 'n' roll and rock 'n' roll instrumentation. Layered on top of that, we have unisex choruses, males and females. And on top of that, we've got a 30-piece orchestra. So it's a hybrid of sound. It's very modern, however, because the BPMs were set at hip-hop speeds and house-music speeds, so we could get into club rotations. I felt that rock 'n' roll wasn't being played in clubs any more, so it was a part of this musical adventure, to bring rock music back into the clubs." Elaborating in an interview with Ultimate-Guitar.com, the project's musical mastermind added that "in this case, there was a combination of writing styles. Many of the beats were programmed alone in my garage initially. In some cases, they were donated by friends who wanted me to co-write tunes. They wanted me to sing on the records. They were programmers - they were like DJ/programmers. It was very much true then, as they say, first and foremost that it was really about the music. It was really about the beat. It was about keeping the house pumping, so to speak. Then from there, I layer rock music with subsonic tones driving through underneath the drums. Any one drum you'll hear is really layered with 3 drum tracks. Then I start to layer on top of it as well with unisex chorusing."

As always, while his latest LP had an impressive roster of collaborators, Perry- in an interview with AVC- clarified that while "its absolutely collaborative...I am the chief solutionist. It's my record. I'm the producer. I'm looking to evolve the concept of the new renaissance artist, taking the world by storm through the art of public display and demonstration, with technical savvy, using cell phones and computers. I go about my business as an artist and I believe that my value is in my product and in my art form, and that's why I can't be stopped, because I began producing this record by myself, without a record company. A record company heard it and liked it a lot, and I was very happy to work with them." Farrell added to Bigshot.com that as he began assembling his guest-player roster for the album, rather than having to lobby anyone, "I didn't actually enlist them, they came to me. They were interested in having me perform for them on their records. Each time, and you can use this as a great excuse if you want to get people to work for you on this scale. I just said, my head is into this great project, Satellite Party, so let's do something unique. Let's split the publishing. Give me your tracks and I'll write lyrics for them and sing for you, but you've just got to leave your tracks with me, and we'll see what happens. The reason I was confident something good was going to happen was because we all come from slightly different worlds. So with Hybrid using my voice, it ended up being more of a remix of what I do, and what I did for their tracks, was I gave them a more radio friendly sound. It's going to get played on rock radio stations, where their music wouldn't have ever gotten on before. So, it worked out really well for us all."

Among Farrell's more prized collaborators included legendary late Doors front man Jim Morrison, whose vocal track for a spoken word composition originally entitled 'Women in the Window' was 30 years old, and a track he conceded to rock journalist Dave Lipp "was a bitch" to put together, adding in an interview with Concert Livewire.com that "after two years of working to get clearance, it all worked out." In the same interview, Perry elaborated on the delicate process of securing rights to use the vocal track, beginning with his recollection that "the Doors have always been good friends of mine, man for years...It was a very large request to have this material hooked up, but they agreed because the story of Satellite Party in part is about a group of people who want to give back to the world, using art to spread the message." Clearly an LP high point for Farrell personally, he happily confessed to the L.A. Times of the opportunity to collaborate with one of his musical heroes that it was special because Morrison and the Doors "epitomized everything that I loved about musicians and music. They were the voice of their generation. They saw things, and they set it to music."

Still, for as joyous as the opportunity to record post-humously with Morrison was, the physical process of creating the song was not without its hick-ups, as Perry recalled to rock journalist Dave Lipp that as he worked from his home studio putting the song together, "what happened was a lot of times the power would go out on us. I swear. Etty's my wife. She can tell you right now. The house would go down. Only our house would go black." The result, as the NY Times later reported, "starts as chill-out music and builds with strings and Beatles allusions while Morrison croons, 'Just try and stop us, we're going to love,' " before gradually building to an orchestral climax that came courtesy of a 30-piece orchestra Farrell added after the fact with the assistance of composer Harry Gregson-Williams, who the singer shared in an interview with Ultimate-Guitar.com"is a film composer who has done The Chronicles Of Narnia, Kingdom Of Heaven, Shrek, Domino, and all of the Tony Scott movies. So he's used to leading 60-piece orchestras. I was working out of his studio. Harry is a good friend and he has a studio - a building, really - in Venice Beach. So while working out of his building, obviously he came down and listened to the music. I wouldn't let him leave until he promised he'd work with me! Harry loves to work on a grand scale, and these film budgets are astronomical. They can run $150 million. So the budget for making music is just so blown out of proportion, it's not funny."

Continuing on the specifics of their collaboration, Farrell added that as they built the orchestral track, "he was composing and making his arrangements on piano. He starts with piano and synthesizer, and then we looked to replace that, his compositions, with the real orchestra. So he was giving me a budget, he put it on paper, and he sent it to me. He said, "*Well, how many pieces do you want?*" I looked at the difference. You can have a 60-piece orchestra. You can have a 30-piece. So I didn't want to have any less than a 15 piece. I looked at it and the jump was just...I mean, I couldn't afford it all! You just don't get those kinds of budgets today in the music business. So I said, "*Well, Harry, what about a 13 piece?*" He went, "*Okay, let's do 15 and I'll get it for the same price.*" So anyway, we were about to do this thing now and we got a very lucky break. There was a 30-piece orchestra that came to town and their gig was canceled. A lot of them are friends of Harry's, and Harry caught wind of this great group of stringed instrumentalists. He told me that it was the greatest assembly of string instrumentalists today. They were all waiting around and he got them together. We got in the studio and set up in their sound studio and recorded all of those songs in one afternoon. We got 5 songs. It's no simple task to conduct 30 people at a time with songs they've never heard before and make it come off right, but Harry did!"

When production moved from Farrell's home studio and Gregson-Williams' neighboring one in Venice to the Village Recorder in West Los Angeles, Mixonline.com reported in June, 2007 that the studio had "recently hosted (an)...album project for Satellite Party...The band— which includes Farrell's wife, Etty, and former Extreme guitarist Nuno Bettencourt— took over several private rooms at The Village while they wrote, tracked, overdubbed, mixed and mastered the project on the Neve consoles in Studios B and D. Ultra Payloaded was produced by Farrell and co-produced and engineered by Bettencourt, with executive producer Steve Lillywhite."

Beginning with his decision to team with Extreme guitarist Nuno Bettencourt, a move that caught EVERYONE who heard the news off guard because of the opposite stylistic backgrounds of Jane's Addiction and Extreme- whose biggest hit was the acoustic pop ballad '*More Than*

Words'- Farrell made the argument that that was precisely why the record's collaborative formula worked as well as it did, explaining to Spin.com that "I love listening to hybrids. I love people that do it all. I'll never not love rock music... But I love working with electronics," adding to Big Shot.com that "for many years I was given a little bit of grief for loving dance music so much from rock 'n' roll people. But I want them to see that dance music has as much energy and impact, and the frequencies they use are so damn rock 'n' roll at times." In recalling specifically how he first joined creative forces with Bettencourt in the studio, Perry shared with Ultimate-Guitar.com that "the first song we worked on was "Milky Ave" and so we had no guitar on it. Not all guitar players know how to respond to music. Many, many people that you'll hear today are very one-dimensional players. They're very green and the music industry is churning out these people really fast. They're not giving them a chance to develop, so a lot of the music that you hear today on radio is very immature in its approach. Nuno, when he began to play, responded to the music. And so, as a result, he added a dimension. Rather than playing, *'Okay, these are the chords. Now I'm going to play right on top of it, the very same chords,'* which you'll hear often today. A great player will say, *'I'm going to respond to those chords.'* As a result, they create a dimension and a melody. It adds dimension, perspective, and everything else. That is magic. That's the magic of musicianship."

That magic extended itself to an inspired all-star cast of guest players indeed, expanding from Jim Morrison and Nuno Bettencourt to include New Order/Joy Division bassist Peter Hook, pioneering electronica act Hybrid, Flea and John Frusciante of the Red Hot Chili Peppers, Silvertide guitarist Nick Perri, and Fergie of the Black Eyes Peas among others. Of the latter collaboration, Perry recalled in an interview with Ultimate-Guitar.com that "through word of mouth did I meet Fergie. A friend who had been listening to the music, a mutual friend, kind of said, *'Listen, I can introduce you to Fergie.'* And so she did, and Fergie came over to my home and hung out with me in my garage along with my wife and Nuno Bettencourt. We just had a little party, put up the tracks, and had a laugh and a drink and sang our hearts out. It was that simple. You can hear it in the sound. It sounds like it's just an enjoyable, relaxed, happy atmosphere. It's not overly processed or overly thought-out."

Hooking up with longtime friend and former fill-in bassist Flea was much more predictable as Farrell recalled, sharing that "Flea I've known forever. Flea and I were running around in L.A. before all of us were really signed. He and I, just before he began to work on and produce *Stadium Arcadium*, he had time on his hands. It was the summertime, so we would go surfing in the morning, have breakfast, and go to each other's houses, just playing songs. I said to him, '*Look, I'm working on this project. I would really love to see what the bass lines would be like and if I got a hold of them and started to produce them using electronic programs.*' So he did. He was very giving and generous with his time and music. He was the first person that I wrote a song with. 'Milky Ave' was the first song." Frusciante's addiction to the project came, as the singer recalled in the same interview with Ultimate-Guitar.com, when "we went over to his house one afternoon and recorded that track live. I took it away and I begged, '*Please, let me just produce this track. Let me just have this track.*' And so he did. He gave the track to me and I ended up obviously producing it and added my voice. Nuno jumped in on the track as well. I brought in my female cohorts, my female vocalists, a drummer, and added programs to it and orchestra to it. So there it is today, this beautiful hybrid of sound again. It sounds like a cross between Jane's Addiction and Chili Peppers."

On completion and release through Sony Records on May 19th, 2007, critics were dazzled, beginning with the L.A. Times' interpretation of Farrell's concept album as one where "Jim Morrison's spirit summons a collective of Internet-savvy artist-activist-environmentalists to slip the surly bonds and attend a party up on high. There, from the vantage point of Morrison's satellite party pad, he invites them to take a break from the wine and revelry for a moment and get a good, long look at the world -- to admire the planet's beauty but also ponder its imminent doom. He shows them the pollution and melting polar ice caps, then sends his party guests back to earth where they are christened as Solutionists and charged with saving the world. That's the concept for the debut album from Perry Farrell's new supergroup, Satellite Party." Mtv.com seemed impressed with the group's success in bringing "to life an indulgent mix of rock, electronic, urban, and symphonic elements that at times resembled a sort of Peter Gabriel-meets-worldbeat sound," while the New York Times got happily lost in the record's "echo-laden Eastern-tinged psychedelia, pulsating new wave, reggae, sinewy punk and especially wah-wah-happy, string-topped 1970s funk, segueing into one another like one of Mr. Farrell's D.J. sets." Billboard, a longtime fan of Perry's craft, seemed most impressed with his songwriting, which they noted in their review was "quite good for this project, and his vocal range is greater than he ever showed with Jane's Addiction or Porno for Pyros," while Spin Magazine concluded that the record successfully achieved what Farrell had sought from the outset: showcasing "the collective's ability to deftly straddle the line between dance pop and edgy rock."

Conclusion : The Next Generation of Jane's Addiction

Following the wrapping of promotional duties for Satellite Party, Perry Farrell turned his attentions back to mainstay Jane's Addiction, who were attempting to make a full-circle return of sorts to their roots by reuniting with founding bassist Eric Avery. Avery's decision to reunite with the band- as he explained to Rolling Stone Magazine in April of

2008- came after much personal deliberation and soul searching, reasoning that initially, "I just didn't like the idea of doing reunions, period. I could only see it as I'd just be going over the same old ground. I'm only years older and fatter and I'll just do an older, fatter version of me. Later I thought more about it and I thought, 'This isn't really different. They aren't asking me to relive some days gone by. They are just saying let's honor the past.' I decided to do it." Acknowledging in the same interview that tensions within the band hadn't entirely subsided with time, the bassist added that "people make it a lot about the interpersonal relationships and there is that sort of tension there, but for me its just about 'Are we good?' We'll take it a step at a time. If we all hate each other, but we're doing great work, okay. I could probably get it done. As long as the work at the end of the day is great. We'll see."

Perry Farrell- who of the band's members had the most personal acrimony with Avery dating back to the group's disbandment in 1991- recalled to Reuters for his own part that, ahead of the reunion, "I just talked to Eric man-to-man. We're different people, that's okay. He serves a different purpose, he's got a different frequency he operates on. I'm overjoyed that we're working together." Following their live performance debut at the NME Awards on April 23rd, 2008, where Jane's was also presented with the Godlike Genius Award- the band by the fall of that year had quietly begun jamming together toward the end of eventually entering the studio to work on new material. Performing their first full set as a reunited foursome at La Cita Bar in their hometown of Los Angeles on October 23rd, 2008, Avery candidly shared of the band's plans going forward that "we never know what the future has in store for us; especially with this band...But, at least right now Jane's Addiction has a future that one would have to call somewhat promising. We are a great band."

Perry Farrell added of the band's future prospects that the band was taking it day-by-day, candidly sharing with MTV.com that "we are at each other's throats almost every step of the way. So the concept of it sounds unbelievable, right? Wow, man — that would be a trip. But then the reality of it starts to set in, and it becomes one of those things where — you know how somebody can just get under your skin and things can just become just unlivable? I go through that process, but let me tell you this. When I think about the party, and I think about the aftereffects, it may be worth it. It may be worth it. But don't hold me to it. It's one of those things, man. I have a fantastic life, and as much as I'd love to have Jane's in my life, I know there's a window. We should try, shouldn't we? We're all still able to kick ass. Musicians, we get good up until we get really old. Our career goes twice as long as an athlete's, but not three times as long. There's a certain age where, all of a sudden, your fingers aren't flying, and you can't jump off the riser anymore, and you can't take your shirt off. So we'll see what happens."

To help referee the reunion as it inevitably gravitated toward the end of creating new music, the band took their typically out-of-the-box approach to just about everything to a new extreme with their decision to enlist Nine Inch Nails mastermind Trent Reznor as co-producer as they entered the studio in the spring of 2009. Recalling how the invitation was formally extended, Reznor- via his website in a February, 2009 blog- shard that "emails were sent, phone calls were made, dinner was arranged, ideas were discussed and the next thing I know we're in the studio experimenting...We laugh, we get to know each other, we cry, we yell, we almost quit, we record LOTS of guitar solos, we discuss, we actually begin to all communicate, we yell some more, we become FRIENDS, we laugh again and we do some great things. I get to see first-hand why they broke up all those years ago but I also get the chance to see four distinct personalities that become an INCREDIBLE band when they're in the same room." Getting their feet wet with a re-record of two classics- 'Chip Away' and 'Whores'- from the band's live XXX debut LP, Perry reasoned of the decision to Billboard that the band went that route "just to get some creative juice flowing- we went into the studio for about two weeks. We had the idea to re-record two tunes, just because they'd never been done officially in the studio. And we had some fun writing some new things. A handful that are close to finished, but not quite done. But there's no rush to put anything out at this point."

By May, 2009, Farrell shared that the sessions had produced two new songs entitled *'Embrace the Darkness'* and *'I'll Protect* You,' with the singer revealing to Billboard that recording with Avery had gotten off to a not-surprisingly rocky start given the band's history, "I'll be honest with you -- we started to record and things got kind of ugly...(Recording) is, like, the last hurdle for us. It's one of those things where the head-butting really came out when we tried to write...The way I look at it is I'm very patient. It's only been, what, 18 years? I can't expect things to be perfect overnight. There's still animosity 'cause it's 18 years' built up. That's just how we roll. But the fact we're all getting back together is a super-positive sign. I know we'll get back in there and write some more...once we've gotten to sit down and have dinner, a couple weeks on the road, get to relax with each other a bit."

While the band toiled away in the studio, they tided fans over with a box set, '*Cabinet of Curiosities*,' released on April 21st, 2009. Critics seemed particularly pleased with the set, with the L.A. Times commenting in their review of the boxset that "its pretty great," while Blabbermouth focused in on the what it felt the true treasure of the set was, noting that while "Jane's Addiction made great albums...its the band's live shows that cemented its legacy. All of the darkness, soul, aggression, and musical zealousness came pouring out night after night as the foursome gelled into a thunderous and dangerous machine." In pouring over a mass of unreleased demos, outtakes and unreleased tracks in the course of assembling the band's first box set, drummer Steven Perkins shared with Billboard that "I supplied a lot of music to Warner Bros. A lot of the stuff has never been heard before," while guitarist Dave Navarro added to the same journalist that "there's some rough sounding stuff, sonically...But it's worth a listen. I have old versions of Zeppelin recordings at home that I don't necessarily throw into rotation all the time, but I like it."

That summer, the band embarked on a co-headlining ampetheatre tour with Nine Inch Nails, performing a set that primarily consisted of highlights from their classic albums, which proved inspiring for both fans and critics alike, beginning with the Miami New Times observation that it felt "as though band and audience were in a time warp," while the Denver Post noted that, though billed as a co-headlining event, "more of the crowd was there for Jane's Addiction," who Austin360.com noted in their review of the band's live set "Austin360.com "was a force of nature." The New York Times, for its part,

"Jane's Addiction looked and sounded uncannily like its old self," while UK's The Guardian added of the band's British live date at Manchester Arena that the band "still sounds both brutal and sensual." Alas, for as well as the group was received by their faithful legions of fans across both the U.S. and Europe, the love wasn't enough to inspire as much within the band's foursome. Though they performed live at the 2009 Voodoo Fest in New Orleans over Halloween weekend and again at the Soundwave Festival in February of 2010, both appearances were merely the band completing contractual obligations with promoters, rather than reflecting a desire to continue playing together.

Bassist Eric Avery clarified the latter loud and clear following the February concert date with his March 3rd announcement via Twitter that "that's it. With equal parts regret and relief, the Jane's Addiction experiment is at an end." Confirming diplomatically via his own Twitter account that "yes, Eric Avery has left the band," guitarist Dave Navarro sought to reassure fans that the band had "more to come," wishing Avery "all the best" in the same time. Farrell- whose bad blood with Avery was a well-documented matter of historic record- was more pointed in his own expression of relief following Avery's departure that the band was, in the process, "slipping out of that shell of a past...Wow we're on to something faster now. And so worth the wait." Adding to Billboard that tensions rose to a head when the band attempted to write new material during sessions with Trent Reznor, the producer candidly recalled that, as that process had gotten underway in-between live dates, "things got kind of ugly...The head-butting really came out when we tried to write." Farrell further shared with Reuters that, indeed, it was the band's creative in-fighting ultimately did the effort in, even as Reznor played the dual roles of producer and referee, offering that "(Trent) did his best to be both producer and psychologist...He was very respectful, trying to get out of the way and not overproduce. I wish honestly he would've produced a little more, but he was a little gun shy after seeing us explode on each other in the studio. He became the referee for a day and after that day I think he was done."

Picking up the pieces yet again, the bond between Farrell, Navarro and Perkins inspired them to carry on with song writing for a new studio album, with Perry sharing with fans via Twitter that stripping back down to basics, "David, Stephen, and I with new writing partner, went into the garage. Felt like old days, except no cassette recorder. Crafting w/Protools." Given the band's penchant for attracting top notch guest bassists like Mike Watt and Flea, speculation ran rampant on the band's fansites and message boards as rumors swirled about the who exactly the band's "new writing partner" was? The answer to that question would turn everyone's heads, not in disbelief, but more the same kind of happy astonishment that had marked the news a few years prior that Soundgarden front man Chris Cornell was joining forces with the members of Rage Against the Machine to form Audioslave or that the members of Guns N' Roses were teaming up with STP front man Scott Weiland to form Velvet Revolver. This time, a member of that troupe was back in the headlines, Duff McKagan, with Slash being among the first to publicly fuel speculation he had replaced Avery as Jane's Addiction's new bassist with his comment to Rolling Stone Magazine re VR's hiatus that "I think Duff is doing something with Jane's Addiction right now so we're all sort of all over the place doing whatever until we can all regroup."

Making their live debut at Farrell's 51st birthday celebration at Les Deux in Los Angeles, California on March 30, 2010, McKagan- in an interview with Spinner.com- revealed the back-story to his decision to join creative forces with the band as having arisen casually over an evening wherein "Perry and I went to dinner with my wife and Etty (Farrell, Perry's wife) and at the end of dinner he said, 'So what are you up to?,' I said, 'Well, I have Loaded working, writing songs.' He says, 'Well, that's kind of what I wanted to talk to you about, writing some songs. Would you be interested in coming in and checking it out?' I was like, 'Yeah, I'll check it out, (but) everything's gotta work great.' He said, 'All of us have been around a long time -- if it doesn't feel right then we know.' Things did feel right." The bassist added in an interview with Jane's Addiction.com that his decision to join the band was motivated in part by the fact that "Slash is going to be touring (behind his new solo album) for at least the next year, and I can't afford to just wait around and see if something's going to happen. These are my years to do something. I'm probably at my peak creatively, and I want to use it. I'm blessed to be able to get that chance now."

The decision to invite McKagan into the band's fold made as much sense to the rest of the band as it did to Farrell, with guitarist Dave Navarro reasoning in an interview with Janesaddiction.com that "we're from the same musical time, the same town, the same era...(so) it was a natural fit," while drummer Steve Perkins added a bit more background to the band's decision in an interview with Music Radar, beginning by sharing that- following the band's 2009 tour- "moving forward is something we all want to do now, but Eric didn't want to move in the same way. I liked playing the old songs on tour, but now it's time to make new music. To do that, the band had to get in a garage or rehearsal studio and get on with it. Perry (Farrell), Dave and I were all on the same page with doing that; Eric wasn't. He didn't feel the same sense of commitment to making new Jane's Addiction music. Obviously, we couldn't force him to do something he doesn't feel, so that's kind of that. We accepted it. You know, there's a thousand great musicians out there to work with, and in the Jane's circle, there's quite a few that we know personally. I've been very fortunate to work with terrific bass players like Flea and Mike Watt. Flea, to me, was a great match in '97. As a drummer, he was very exciting for me to work with. But he doesn't play with a pick, so to bring him back into Jane's...well, he can't replicate Eric; nobody can. It was time for us to move in a different way. We have to evolve...A lot of things contributed to the process. Dave and Duff have done a lot of shows with Camp Freddy [the side project led by Velvet Revolver drummer Matt Sorum], and they got on well. Last year, I participated in an instructional DVD about how drummers and bass players interact. For some cosmic reason, Duff and I chose each other and we sat in front of the camera and did a couple of things. At the same time, Perry started hanging out with Duff. So like I said, it was synchronicity; it all fell into place without us trying to make it happen. Rather than us looking around for a bass player or taking out ads or something, the obvious choice was right there...We discussed a few different bass players, but suddenly Duff came into our lives...Of course, we've known Duff for quite a while, even going back to his GN'R days. We never viewed Guns N' Roses as competition or anything. Back in the day, Jane's was always hanging out with the Chili Peppers and Fishbone and bands like that, whereas GN'R were a bit more on the Sunset Strip...It was almost like synchronicity. We had a jam or two and it felt great, so we found ourselves all saying, 'OK, why don't we do this?'"

For McKagan, a big attraction- aside from Velvet Revolver's hiatus- for joining the band came with "a chance to write, record and perhaps even perform with a band of the quality of Jane's Addiction," further sharing in his Seattle Weekly blog that such an opportunity "does not come around every day. I have a lot of respect for this band and the guys in it. The music that we have been writing is an extension of that mutual respect...I have been a huge fan of Eric Avery since the mid-'80s, when I would go to see them play at clubs down in L.A. This is not, in my mind, about me replacing him, in any way shape or form. I have a lot of respect for this band and the guys in it. The music that we have been writing is an extension of that mutual respect. AND it's a blast! Perry Farrell is an absolute visionary. Dave Navarro has always been a guitar player who I have had a lot of respect for. Playing in a rhythm section with Stephen Perkins is almost trancelike. Kick-ass for sure. I also want to make it clear to JA fans that I really appreciate all of the kind words and sentiment directed to me."

By May 6th, Rolling Stone Magazine reported that "Jane's Addiction had special reason to celebrate Cinco de Mayo on Wednesday night, performing for the first time with new bassist Duff McKagan for an intimate crowd of fans and friends in Hollywood. 'Gn'R and Jane's Addiction rose from adjacent corners of the mid-'80s hard-rock scenes of Los Angeles, and both were veterans of the notorious and influential underground club the Scream. Onstage with Jane's in 2010, McKagan set a thick, watery bassline against Navarro's speedy solo on '*Whores*' (from 1987), and it sounded like a collaboration built to last." Back in the studio, McKagan described a working atmosphere that stood in almost complete contrast to that the band had faced with Avery, sharing with Janesaddiction.com that because "I don't have years of history with this band...there's no like, 'Oh, what happened to that chick in 1989?' still twenty-fucking-five years later. Everything's been great...I've never been in a band I wasn't in from the beginning...So to play songs like 'Been Caught Stealing' is pretty fucking kickass."

Elaborating on his process of blending musically into the band's sound, the bassist- courtesy of a May 20, 2010 blog for the Seattle Times entitled 'Learning the Old Jane's Addiction Jams', began by sharing with fans that "never before have I been in a situation where I had to play bass lines written by someone else for a whole set. It is a challenge for sure, and an eye-opening experience as far as pushing my style in a different direction. On June 9 and 11, I will be playing two European shows with Jane's Addiction. These gigs come at a time when we have been writing new songs for a while, and it's a chance to get outside the studio and sort of shake off the dust. But first I had to learn some of their old catalogue. In all the bands I've been in, we have always done covers of other artists. GNR did Dylan's *'Knockin' on Heaven's Door'* and *'Mama Kin'* by Aerosmith. Neurotic Outsiders did *'New Rose'* by the Damned; VR did *'Surrender'* by Cheap Trick and *'Wish You Were Here'* by Pink Floyd. And Loaded has done everything from *'TNT'* by AC/DC to *'Purple Rain'* by Prince. But all these covers were played by bands I had already been playing with for some time. They were simply our interpretations of these songs ... good or bad. A couple of weeks ago, as I was in the Jane's rehearsal room going through a set of JA classics, I found myself feeling really uncomfortable and unsettled. I couldn't figure it out. Was my bass rig not sounding right? Could I not hear Steven Perkins' bass drum well enough? Was I playing in the right groove and at the right volume? These are not things one should be thinking while playing. You should be in the moment and let things flow. And suddenly it dawned on me: I was playing bass parts for a whole set of songs that were written by someone else WITH the band that had recorded them. Oh ... this is new!"

Continuing, it was clear that McKagan was aware of the great tradition of bass players he was now officially part of, paying homage in his blog first and foremost to his predecessor, commenting that "Eric Avery, was always a guy whom I very much respected as a bass player. Back in the mid-'80s club days in L.A., I remember going to see JA just to watch Avery and Perkins. The way they interwove rhythm was ridiculous, and a bit groundbreaking. For some reason over the years, he and I never actually met. This added to his mystique for me. So now as I am playing some of those bass lines, I feel the pressure that I perceive is probably out there. You know: Everyone will be looking at ME to see how I play those beloved bass lines, an integral part of the JA sound. Really good bass players are a very rare thing in rock music. James Jamerson and Donald 'Duck' Dunn from the Motown and Stax Records days set a high-water mark that has only been just touched upon since then. John Paul Jones of Led Zeppelin borrowed heavily from those two, but then added a lot of his own mojo and passed it forward for anyone else to try and improve on. Eric Avery and Robert DeLeo (from Stone Temple Pilots) have probably been the closest as far as carrying on JPJ's lineage, and this is meant as a huge compliment. Paul Simonon from the Clash set the tone for me, as far as modern-day bass players go. He has such a killer sense of pocket and style. Randy Rampage from DOA and Simonon were for sure the two bassists who I chose to follow and mimic when I decided to switch from guitar to the four-strings in 1984. Some of the great bass players from the post-'70s punk and noise era introduced more of a mood, almost a sense of color, to stereos around the world. Raven from Killing Joke is a good example of where the actual playing is not the thing that gets you; it's the attitude in which it's played that makes you want to break shit. Krist Novoselic is a monster player too. Guys who I know and play with realize what a huge part he had in Nirvana's makeup. Without Krist being the aggressive and melodic player that he is and was, those records would have been oh-so-much different. You can actually hear his style develop and mature from *Bleach* to *Nevermind* to *In Utero*. I like it when I can hear and recognize a player getting better. I feel like I am somehow a part of it. OK. So here I am, playing older Jane's songs and trying to be true to those bass lines while trying to infuse some of my own thing (whatever THAT is!). We are writing new songs, and I can only hope to leave my mark somehow and not do any damage to this great legacy. At the end of the day, I still love what I do and am lucky to make a living at a thing that is also my passion."

Commenting from a drummer's perspective on working in yet another new bass player to the Jane's fold, drummer Steve Perkins shared with Musicradar.com, from the beginning, "the idea of having Duff in the band struck us as fucking cool. He's a great guy. He plays in his own way. I think it's an interesting hybrid. I don't like to use the word 'flashy,' but Dave and I are inspired by a lot of notes, whereas Duff comes from more of a straightforward punk-rock school of playing. It's a cool clash of styles, I think. We feel really together now as a band, very unified, and there's a lot of fresh energy...The work ethic has been fantastic. He's definitely here for us when we need him, no question. He gets in the room with us and works out songs, then he takes tapes home - he's there. He's been a nice shot of vitamin B. It's been really cool and a lot of fun. I'm more of a spastic kind of Keith Moon-type player, and Duff is very rough and tough. There's less notes but he plays with authority. It's like sandpaper on sandpaper, but it's working out fine. He's got great ears and he knows how to hook in with me. We're finding ourselves again, and it's exciting. Even playing older songs like Mountain Song, it feels new again. Duff approaches it more like a rhythm guitar player. It's going to sound different to a lot of people, but maybe they'll appreciate it on a new level...Duff knows how fragile bands are. But he's in for the ride, I know that He's one of us. Jane's Addiction is now the four of us: Perry, Dave, Duff and myself. Duff's a full-time member and he's ready to bite off as much as we are. What that ultimately means for the future of Velvet Revolver, I don't know."

As the summer of 2010 progressed along with the band's studio writing, Duff updated fans via an interview with Spinner.com that "we recorded three songs a couple weeks ago and it sounds huge, dynamic. (We) went and played a couple of shows in Europe and it was really fun. I had a great time playing with Perry. (They're) really good guys to travel with. I'm having a fucking blast. This is like rock royalty, Jane's, People want that old-school original because a lot of rock music right now is so paint-by-numbers. It's bland, really bland. I've heard some songs on the radio. I'm like, 'You gotta be fucking kidding me.' At least where I come from that's not good. That's not fucking good." Well rehearsed by this point as a four-piece, the bassist added in an interview with Janesaddiction.com that songwriting was "97 percent of what our time is geared towards," adding of the process of blending his songwriting process with that of the band's that "when I first sent some songs to Perry they were the in the usual style that I write music — verse, chorus, chorus, bridge, double chorus, etc. If you listen to a great Jane's Addiction song, though, there's no chorus! It's just riff, and then it goes into some psychedelic jam. I've had to learn to sort of adapt as a songwriter. I just have to bring in a riff. Some snarling, mean, dark and dismal riff, that's going to be our thing."

Unfortunately, by the early fall of 2010, the tide had turned for what seemed had become the band's smoothest sailing in years as news broke nationally across the media waves that the band and their new bassist were parting company. Depending on the headline- whether you read MSNBC.com's headline that 'Ex-Guns N' Roses bassist leaves Jane's Addiction' or Blabbermouth.net's that 'Jane's Addiction Parts Ways with Duff McKagan,' the result was the same: Jane's Addiction was again bassless. The band, for its part, issued an explanation from their official website that again blamed creative differences for McKagan's departure, diplomatically beginning by stating that "we wanted to thank Duff for helping us write songs for our new record. We love the songs we worked on with him - and the gigs were a blast - but musically we were all headed in different directions. From here Duff is off to work on his own stuff so we wish him all the best." Perry Farrell wished McKagan well from his Twitter account by stating that "Jane's wishes Duff much luck with his band Loaded. What a fun time we all had working together. Look out for his record and tour this fall." Commenting individually on the bassist's departure from the band's fold, guitarist Dave Navarro complimented McKagan on his creative contributions to the band's latest writing efforts by sharing with Blabbermouth.net his opinion that "Duff's an amazing writer and an amazing player. At the end of the day, I think his band, Velvet Revolver, is trying to get their thing back together and they're auditioning singers. So we wish him the best with that. . . As far a (new) bass player, we don't really have anybody right now in mind. The three of us — Perry, Stephen, and myself — are writing and hashing out the songs."

Regardless of how Jane's Addiction's future music plans wind up panning out, their legacy as what Popmatters.com hailed as "truly the closest our generation has come to having its own Led Zeppelin" is secured. Looking back over the mainstream alternative rock movement that band visionary Perry Farrell founded a quarter-century ago, critics like the Los Angeles Times have qualified the latter with their conclusion that that the Jane's front man "wasn't just the physical embodiment of alt rock but its main proponent, elevating it to the sound that defined a decade," while MTV recently added that "Perry Farrell is, quite simply, one of the most important and original musical figures." Popmatters.com, for its part, has concluded in measuring the historic expanse of the band's influence in shaping the aforementioned genre that "(Jane's Addiction) forged ahead with its unique blend of musical influences, laying the groundwork for the genre that would become known as alternative. The importance of Jane's Addiction to the germination of '90s music is a given," adding in similar acknowledgement to the latter critics that "Farrell's writing and vision had always been the guiding force behind the band's recorded successes."

As relevant to sustaining the viability of the alternative rock genre in 2010 as they were in launching it 25 years ago, Jane's Addiction will without a doubt continue to inspire the genre's future generations as they focus on their next studio LP. Looking to the future with his mainstay band- who in 2010 the BBC concluded had reached the status of "legendary"- front man Perry Farrell recently shared in a Fall, 2010 interview with Big Shot.com that "with Jane's Addiction, we're in writing mode, and I'm working with Rich Costey as a producer who has done Muse and Rage Against The Machine. He's kind of a hybrid producer, and we're hoping to have a record out early next year. We have tracks that we've already finished, and probably 20 more that we haven't yet...(Soon) we go into the studio again to record more tracks!"

BONUS SAMPLER

(Featuring bands from around the world performing original music inspired by that of Jane's Addiction)

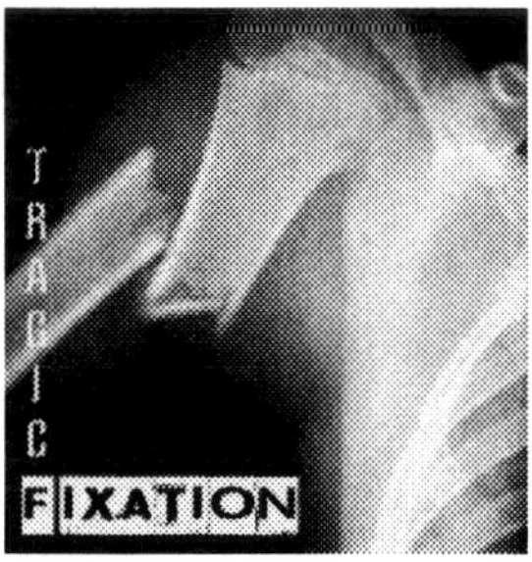

In 2010, Tragic Fixation finally put all the pieces together. Denver music scene veterans Dave Gaskill (keyboards, sequencing) and Cory Jones (guitars, sequencing) have joined forces with CR Payne (former voice of the BloodSuit) to create an aggressive and diverse brand of original industrial sound. Pushing the boarders of their genre, the trio has drawn upon influences from the past and present that converge as an unrelenting collection of songs and live performances. Sophisticated rhythms and well-structured songs create the framework for uniquely crafted lyricism, all of which are enhanced by a visually stimulating and intelligent stage show. Dark, moody and often angry, the atmosphere surrounding TF engulfs the senses of listeners, and, as one verse shouts, "Leave(s) a mark so they'll remember". A three song demo can be found at: www.soundclick.com/tragicfixation

Broken Glow is a rock band out of New York City. With a taste for all of rock's genres, Broken Glow has a created a sound uniquely their own. They're currently playing around the North East and working on their debut album. Check out www.Myspace.com/BrokenGlow for any current info and show locations.

Sunsets North- Fronted by the creative talent and breath taking vocals of Warren North, the band brings a dynamic and alternative twist of original music that's loaded with synthesizers, subtle yet poignant effects, and strong heart melting harmonies. SunSets North would not be complete without North's loyal sidekicks

Shane Riling, Pete Quinter & Derrick Stair. All three were handpicked by North, Riling for his ripping solos and filling guitar styles, Stair for his monstrous bass skills and catchy harmonies and Quinter for his unforgettable performances, unstoppable fills and dynamic samples. Their live sets are presented with the same high energy that is born from the same passion that brought you their music. With an extraordinary sound and engaging live shows, they are one band that shouldn't be overlooked. With music that is powerful and expressive, as well as audibly unique, their new CD will have you gasping for more! Thank you, Warren North 610.390.7639 begin_of_the_skype_highlighting 610.390.7639 end_of_the_skype_ highlighting SunSets North myspace.com/sunsetsnorth

No Regime is an Alternative Punk Rock band that embraces ska, reggae and latin music in their songs. Their music focuses on social life and political issues. The band formed in early 2009 in Los Angeles, CA and the line up consists of Jason Rea on Vocals, Enrique Suárez on Guitar, Andy Zamora on Drums and Marc Pardy on bass. No Regime started to perform actively in Southern California after recording their first demo which featured 4 songs. One of the songs from this demo "Anguish" was featured on the Urban Shit Records compilation, a DIY label from the S.F. Valley in California and also on a UCLA Unsigned Bands compilation. In February 2010, their first EP was released featuring 6 songs, getting positive reviews from industry professionals and respected punk related online websites. This EP is available to download for free via their myspace page. Some of the songs from this E.P. including "Anguish" and "Mr. Frilles" are constantly being played on online radio stations. In March 2010, vocalist Jason Rea enters the band replacing Jake Yoshizaki. During the 2010 summer, the song “Anguish”, featuring Jason Rea on vocals, was selected to be part of the “Jane’s Addiction: In the Studio” Book Bonus Sampler released by Rock n’ Roll Books. In addition to that, the band shot their first music video for the song “Anguish” in Los Angeles, CA. The video was directed by Andres Arango and features Jason on vocals. In August 2010, no Regime was a semifinalist on a Hard Rock Café competition in Las Vegas, NV, after defeating more than 20 national bands. The band has being performing different venues and events such as the Quiet Rebel Films Fundraiser, organized by this film production company based in Los Angeles, the famous Etnies Skate Park in Orange County, CA, the ¨Best Rock Night in Hollywood¨ according to the Los Angeles Times at Cinespace in Hollywood among others. The band has been writing new music, preparing the release of a new E.P. with Jason on vocals, increasing their fan base and continuously performing in Southern California. No Regime pride themselves on their distinguished, intense and energetic live performances. Visit the band online at

MONGREL is an aggressive rock band with punk and metal influences for fans of bands such as Guns N' Roses, Misfits, Jane's Addiction, Amen, System of a Down, old Metallica, etc.. Called "the hardest working band in Boston" (Metal Edge), Mongrel has played with bands such the Misfits, Korn, GWAR, Fu Manchu, Fear, Otep, Prong, etc. and received steady airplay on Sirius/XM and Music Choice. With new vocalist Jessica Sierra, Mongrel has recorded their latest EP "The New Breed of Old School" as a reintroduction of 6 fan favorite songs from their first full length album "Fear, Lies, & Propaganda". Mongrel will be re-entering the studio to record their next full length cd for a Spring 2011 release. For more songs, upcoming show info, etc

please visit www.MongrelBand.com or contact the band at mongrelBand@yahoo.com. Mongrel - aggressive punk/rock/metal
http://www.MongrelBand.com,http://www.myspace.com/Mongrel,
http://www.facebook.com/MongrelBand,
http://www.twitter.com/MongrelBand,
http://www.reverbnation.com/MongrelBand,
http://www.vimeo.com/Mongrel,
http://www.youtube.com/adamMongrel,
http://www.airplaydirect.com/Mongrel, or
http://www.sonicbids.com/Mongrel

Waiting for Decay- here must be something about the heat of the desert that makes the music sound so sweet. SoCals High Desert acoustic band, Waiting for Decay (WFD), has been banging out the tunes on the stage and on the airwaves for four years now. Starting as a coffee shop side project for metal vocalist Dewayne Clifton, the acoustic approach progressed into a full fledged rock band that can rival most hardcore groups, but still appeal to larger radio friendly audience. Turning the heads and ears of thousands of fans across the globe, WFDs style of music branches from soulful ballads to the full scream of metal. Backed by guitarists Michael Zepol , Bassist Dan Bartlett, and percussionist James Cottrell, the music is blended with a wide range of influences. Trickles of country, blues, bluegrass, flamenco, metal, and good ole rock and roll find their way into this ecliptic mix. WFD has been on the interview circuit and showcased on hundreds of Pod-casts, traditional, internet and Sirius Satellite radio programs. Having performed on bills ranging from singer songwriters showcases, coffee shop venues, to Sunset Strip clubs (Viper Room, Roxy, Cat Club, etc), WFD can fit any type of booking. While still holding on to the traditional purity of acoustic music, Waiting for Decay has adapted a Rock Show attitude whenever they perform. Bringing audiences to the edge of their seat and holding them there for the entire show. Whether interacting with WFD fans on Myspace, or at any show, one thing is clear, WFD will grab you and will not let go. Visit the band online at www.myspace.com/waitingfordecay

Division Within- "Sometimes you need to walk with death to know why you're alive." For Richard Zandlo, founder and rhythm guitarist of Division Within, a rock/melodic metal group from Phoenix, AZ, walking with death was a life long experience. Born with Cystic Fibrosis, a genetic lung disease that leads to life-threatening lung infections, music was the impetus for his life. Division Within was formed in 2008 by Zandlo and Drummer Brian "Monster" Elam with a simple concept: Heavy music, Heavy emotion. The industry is filled with talented musicians and the only way to stand out is be true to yourself. "The music is who we are." Their concept was immediately met with local success as they quickly garnered fans and began to open for national bands. Their momentum halted when Zandlo's deteriorating condition forced the band to go on hiatus. "The band was dissolving. We had just lost our vocalist, lead guitarist, and bassist. With Rich's health deteriorating, nothing seemed to be going right.", recalls Elam. In December of 2009, everything changed; Zandlo received a double-lung transplant granting the guitarist a new lease on life and the band re-emerged with renewed energy and focus. "Everyday is a blessing. I want everyone to feel what I feel through our music". This 5-piece features guitarist Richard Zandlo, Brian "Monster" Elam on drums, Michael Logan on vocals, lead guitarist Tommy Wray, and bassist Adam Fay. Division Within has formulated their own unique mix of modern metal with a melodic twist that has energized fans across the region. Having performed numerous shows, ultimately prepared them to open shows for Tantric, Burn Halo, and Adema. After an inauspicious beginning, Division Within's future looks promising with no signs of slowing down. In 2010, they released their first EP "Last Chance", a three track sampling of their dynamic original sound. The first single, "Shut Up and Bleed" is a heavy melodic-metal tune that is sure to ignite music fans and their future.

Universal Debris thanks and celebrates the numerous forms of blockage that exist completely and the enduring process of tactically humorizing the most adverse and uncomfortable situation or condition. Without the collective blockage, there would be no recognition on such a massive scale that an explanatory description could not be accurately applied as an absolute basis for understanding. Universal Debris is in the way here.AND over there. Centered in and around VENICE, CA. Universal Debris is devised by JonJacobsen (JonJ) who came to Los Angeles in from San Francisco in 1986 where he enjoyed the 80's punk and metal movements and started a band called Potential ThreatSF who have enjoyed global appreciation. The Los Angeles music scene picked up from 1986 on and witnessed many local shows with Red Hot Chili Peppers, Fishbone and Janes Addiction at the Variety Arts Club, Scream and Rajii's.. He quickly took up playing bass and learning much from 2 cuban families who's members were a group of musicians and played from 1987 - 1992. A further journey into African styles of music led to performances with one group led by Nigerian master percussionist Ayo Adeyemi and with up to 20 players. Jon went on to form an experimental rock project in the 90's called Dreadful Lemon Sky which acheived local recognition and local radio Airplay on KXLU and public access television. He also subbed on bass for the early Black Eyed Peas and performed with band Mary Mother Jones.In 2003 JJ played with Guvner including members of Bang Tango and Producer Robbie Nevil until disbanding in 05 due to musical differences. It wasn't until 2005 that JJ started writing lyrics and melody then music parts and programming drums. He wrote for about 4 years building a collection of complete songs and now continues improving in producing and writing and is preparing for Universal Debris live shows. Many musicians are involved with Universal Debris including Bassist, Dickie Bruce, Drummer Brian Sumwalt, Guitarist Reggie Davis, Guitarist Mark Latham, Drummer Dave Krusen, Freestlyist Myka 9. JJ is also co owner of JB Music Company with Partner Hawkeye Bronstein; focusing on scoring media and entertainment. Universal Debris has released one full length album and three singles on itunes in 2010. One being a cover song of Massive Attack "Protection" which is a favorite. Universal Debris is parented by Pedestal Industries who's initial product offering, The Pedestal is now available on-line and in finer adult novelty boutiques in the US and Internationally.

Circadian clock is a young but experienced four piece rock band with intensive classical training. Officially formed in September 2008, the band's progress has been rapid. While the mix of styles when heard weaves together the influences of Latin music, funk, classical and rock, at a first glance, the band is a seemingly randomly assembled group of perfect strangers. A punk Black and Japanese violinist who wants to be a singer (Vile), a strong Puerto Rican drummer (Wes), a polka loving Mexican bassist video game nerd (Charlemagne), and an anime obsessed hyperactive classical pianist(Ayumi), at no point seem to share anything in common. But there is love in this deep friendship, and the greatest love shared between them is a love for music. It all started by chance, or perhaps fate, when Wes and Vile attended the same music summer camp, began a discussion about Vile's gothic pants, and after several years became best friends. Charlemagne was by chance sitting on a rock and playing bass, and happened to become an irreplaceable asset to the band. Wes, continuing to attend music camp, found Ayumi for an (unfairly difficult) recording, and by fate we all ended up becoming close. Talented, young, classically trained and driven, a goal has been set up by Circadian, and it will be met. "Niche? They want us to appeal to a niche? They simply then don't know what we do. What is it that we do? We do what we want!" - Ayumi, Keys.

Oak Street Blues is an Alternative Folk/Country band. Founded by Chris Hall, a veteran of several bands spanning genres as diverse as Gangsta Rap to Electronica to Rockabilly and back again, the sound of Oak Street Blues is the true definition of what makes a man crazy about women,

heartbreak, and '55 Buicks. Once he was satisfied with the direction of the music, he enlisted two of his friends to join the ranks; Jon Meier on Bass, and James Vela on keyboards. To complete the band, an ad calling for a drummer was answered by Alejandra Arellano. The sound is energetic, lively, and unpredictable. Live shows have proven that any audience can immediately become immersed with the sounds of an alternative cover of "I Think We're Alone Now", as well as a syrupy sweet, country-tinged "Sugartown" (complete with a Kazoo-along), mixed with all original songs about pumpkins, and longing for a night lost in an unrequited love's eyes. Oak Street Blues is currently recording new material and playing live shows all over Los Angeles as the "For Lovers Only" tour continues into the summer of 2010. Head to www.oakstreetblues.com

Based out of Chicago, IL, Devil's Candy's influences include Primus, Jane's Addiction, and the Red Hot Chili Peppers among others. Visit the band online at http://www.myspace.com/devilscandymusic

Sean Ozz - Vocals / Bass / Keyboard
Ronnie Kopal - Bass / Guitar
Dave Swetnam - Drums

They have had ambitions and dreams of playing live and sharing their music, their art with people since each picked up their 1st instrument.... Though life had gotten in the way time and time again they have all come together now with talent, hard work, dedication, and life experience to bring a unique sound into the world. The band boasts a variety of influences including The

Cure, Janes Addiction, BauHaus, Joy Division, Radiohead, Stranger than Fiction, Smashing Pumpkins, Deftones, and Tool. Visit them online at http://myspace.com/theabyss

Based out of Nashville, Tennessee, members of The Opposed bring a culmination of styles from their various backgrounds into a unique and progressive, yet accessible sound that is powerful and intense. The groundwork is laid with heavy riffs from guitarist Roland Price (with influences of Metallica and Eric Johnson) and bassist Cj Wheeler (with influences of As I Lay Dying and Animals As Leaders) punctuated with the soulful blues stylings of guitarist Dean Sizemore (influenced by Neal Schon and Joe Perry). Atop this foundation sits drummer Edwin Rivera III (influenced by Mike Portnoy and various R&B artists) with intricate but tasteful flare that accentuates the groove set by the guitars. With soaring melodies and powerful lyrics, Matt Singleton (with influences like Chris Cornell and Myles Kennedy) weaves into the mix with intensity that hooks on and never lets go, tying their sound together into a unique and cohesive style. The Opposed consists of professional musicians dedicated to their craft, and to them, it is more than a band. It is a platform for the passion to influence and change the lives that they encounter. Visit the band online at *www.**myspace**.com/**opposed**4jesus*

Canada-based singer/songwriter and lead vocalist Rose Reiter cannot be stylistically confined to any one genre, with a voice that ranges as broadly across the sonic spectrum of styles as her pallet of influences, which run from Annie Lennox, Peter Gabriel, Sarah McLachlan and Sade all the way to Led Zeppelin, Genesis, Pink Floyd, and Stevie Wonder. Rose has appeared on numerous compilations distributed world-wide, including Tribute Lps to Tina Turner, Kiss, Led Zeppelin, and Guns N' Roses, along with solo album releases including 2002's '*What I Don't Get*' and 2006's '*REal.*' Reiter also fronts rock/dance hybrid act Skyscreamers, whose debut LP is due in stores in mid-2011 from Millennium Vinyl Records/MVD. Her equal focus is composing songs for TV /Film, and has many of her songs available on Itunes, Amazon, and wherever digital releases are found. www.rosereiter.com She works with her partner in life and music, Gerry Plant. Find them both at www.plantshop.ca Check her out at www.myspace.com/rosereiter, www.rosereiter.com, or www.myspace.com/skyscreamers

NYC-based artist and lead guitarist Alex Schuchard first picked up his dad's Paul Reid Smith at age 11, and has been strumming ever since, bringing an eclectic style of playing that blends alt-and-70's classic rock into a sound that reflects influences ranging from Jane's Addiction and the Pixies all the way to the Rolling Stones and The White Stripes. Schuchard also runs the critically-acclaimed Space B Art Gallery in New York's Chelsea District. Schuchard's guitar work can soon be heard more elaborately on his band Skyscreamers' debut LP, due in mid-2011 from Millennium Vinyl Records/MVD. Check out his work online at spaceb.com

Producer/rhythm keeper Jake Brown, who rounds out the line-up on drums (live and programmed), keyboards, bass and related instrumentation, brings a rock/industrial-electronica hybrid of influences to the project, including Ministry, Beck, Siouxsie and the Banshees, Trent Reznor, Morcheeba, Dr. Dre, the Sugar Cubes, Prince, NIN, Jane's Addiction, Sonic Youth, the Cowboy Junkies, and a host of other influences. As a record producer, Brown's other forthcoming projects include a star-studded Dr. Dre Tribute LP, the UFOlogy-themed industrial/electronica project 'The Conspiracy Channel' (www.myspace.com/theconspiracychannel), and art-rock/trip hop concept project 'The Haunted Heads' (www.myspace.com/thehauntedheads), mixing duties on Leaving Eden's forthcoming studio LP, as producer/performer on his own band Skyscreamers' debut LP, due in the mid-spring, 2011 from Millennium Vinyl Records/MVD, and as producer on the forthcoming 'The Chronic 2011: A Tribute to the Songs of Dr. Dre,' due in 2011. Brown has also workrd for the last 8 years as a music biographer, with 25 published books to his resume (including authorized titles with Heart, Motorhead, the Meat Puppets, Rick James, 2Pac, founding GNR guitarist Tracii Guns, former adult film star Jasmin St. Claire, and others). Visit brown online at www.jakebrownbooks.com

Anatomy of Sound - Picture this, four crazy scientists dissecting sound form down to its molecular state hoping to find something deeper within a hearer's sensation. Envision life as their root to all equations solving puzzles one step at a time. Imagine a four piece band rooting their inspirations from greats like Bach, Pink Floyd, and Einstein.......Wait a second.....Einstein!!!!..... He didn't compose music! What are you talking about! Alright scratch that fancy beginning; Believe it or not, there is no crazy story line with events that make you fall of your seat from sitting on the edge. No twist in the plot or out of the world irony and no jaw-dropping cliff ending that occur, mostly due to the fact that there is no ending in sight. The past is inevitable. People and places are in constant symmetry creating life-altering events. Being mainly middle school hooligans, Anatomy of Sound met each other in a local church where friendships spur. Four young kids spent their time fighting forces of good and evil. Learning life values with sun setting stories of pranks, they didn't even consider playing music. Not too many nights and days passed when simple ideas turned in to action. The four of them have found each other in the mist of their community church with music in their hearts and instruments in their hands. The future has cracked its door open. Anatomy of Sound was officially formed March 2007 A.D. with faith in something greater than can be captivated or even seen.... faith in the future... The four of friends to this day battle good vs. evil within themselves as their moral values collide with life's simple pleasures. This classic theme that drives their inner struggle of humanity became the premises of Anatomy of Sound's lyrical foundation. Unified ideas have created an indestructible chemistry within the members as the story begins to unfold....... Visit the band online at www.myspace.com/theanatomyofsound

Visit www.rocknrollbooks.com to download free bonus sampler:

Tracklisting

1. Mongrel - **Shut Up, Get Dead**
2. Broken Glow - **Dogs & Demons**
3. Skyscreamers - **Tribe**
4. Universal Debris - **How About That**
5. Sunsets North - **Goodbye Syndrome**
6. Tragic Fixation - **Oversized**
7. No Regime - **Anguish**
8. Sunsets North - **Break the Mold**
9. Waiting for Decay - **Mask or Face**
10. The Abyss - **Beautiful Lie**
11. Division Within - **Shut Up and Bleed**
12. Universal Debris - **Safe and Sane**
13. Circadian Clock - **Ashes in the Dust**
14. Oak Street Blues - **Don't You Know**
15. Devil's Candy - **Funk Your Mutha**
16. The Abyss - **Shattered Dreams**
17. Anatomy of Sound - **Despirator**
18. The Opposed - **Mr. Optimus**

About the Author

Nashville-based biographer is the author of thirty published books, including 'Motorhead: In the Studio' (co-written with Lemmy Kilmister), founding Guns N' Roses guitarist Tracii Guns authorized memoir, due in summer, 2011; 'Tom Waits: in the Studio' (due June, 2011), 'AC/DC in the Studio', 'Heart: in the Studio' (co-written with Ann and Nancy Wilson), 'Tori Amos: in the Studio' (due June, 2011), 'Rick Rubin: In the Studio,' 'Dr. Dre: In the Studio,' 'Suge Knight: The Rise, Fall and Rise of Death Row Records,' '50 Cent: No Holds Barred,' 'Biggie Smalls: Ready to Die,' 'Tupac: In the Studio' (authorized by the estate), as well as titles on Kanye West, R. Kelly, Jay-Z, the Black Eyed Peas, and non-hip hop titles including 'An Education in Rebellion: The Biography of Nikki Sixx,' 'Red Hot Chili Peppers: In the Studio,' 'Alice in Chains: In the Studio,' 'Meat Puppets: In the Studio' (co-written with Curt and Cris Kirkwood, due June, 2011), and the Behind the Boards Rock Producers Anthology Series. Brown is also a featured author in Rick James' autobiography, 'Memoirs of Rick James: Confessions of a Super Freak, and is the co-author of 'What the Hell Was I Thinking?!!,' the authorized memoir by former adult film star Jasmin St. Claire (due, Oct. 2010). In February 2008, Brown appeared as the official biographer of record on Fuse TV's Live Through

This: Nikki Sixx TV special and Bloomberg TV's forthcoming Jay Z special. Brown has received additional press in national publications including USA TODAY, MTV.com, The New York Post, Vibe, NPR, Billboard, Revolver, the San Francisco Chronicle, and Publishers Weekly. Brown was recently nominated alongside Lemmy Kilmister for the 2010 Association for Recorded Sound Collections Awards in the category of Excellence in Historical Recorded Sound Research.

IN STORES NOW FROM ROCK N ROLL BOOKS:

'An Education in Rebellion : The Biography of Nikki Sixx'
(ISBN 9780972614252)

'Alice in Chains: in the Studio'
(ISBN 9780972614269)

Coming in 2011:

'Prince: in the Studio - The Hits 1975-1995'

(ISBN: 978-0-9726142-4-5)